Surveys and Scams

A Chronicle of American Life

[signature: Kirk Andersen]

KIRK ANDERSEN

Here's my new book! Read it and tell me what you think about it.

Copyright © 2022 Kirk Andersen
All rights reserved
First Edition

PAGE PUBLISHING
Conneaut Lake, PA

First originally published by Page Publishing 2022

ISBN 978-1-6624-8688-3 (pbk)
ISBN 978-1-6624-8697-5 (digital)

Printed in the United States of America

To my mom who has always given me love and support and has been a "friend of the mind" to me.

Security is mostly a superstition. The majority of mankind never experience it; life is an adventure and should be treated as one.

—Helen Keller

Contents

1. The Non-Person 1
2. The White Supremacists League 15
3. Survey Today, Scam Tomorrow 30
4. Videohead 42
5. A Conspiracy of Charlatans 54
6. The Hard-liners 69
7. The Dripping Faucet 82
8. The Clerk Job 89
9. Podunk Hill 97
10. Apotheosis 112
11. Daybreak at Fort Jackson 120
12. Fallout Shelter 126

The Non-Person

The streetlights were humming as he made his way down the dark street, passing each equidistant light hub with a solemnity that he carried in his small frame. The cars passed by with headlights that beamed a lonely glow into the darkening evening's entourage of traffic. There weren't too many people out on the streets this late, but he felt a wave of fear grip him at points when he walked under the shadow of some of the city's buildings and passed by the dark splotches of deserted lots.

It was when he reached the flashing parking garage sign that Raymond Delosis knew he had found his contact. The sign said "park here" on and off again in the city's darkness, and he saw the figure of a man in the booth behind it. He waved at him, and the man gave a nod of compliance. Raymond walked up to the booth and knocked on the window. The man opened it and stated, "Are you here for the custodial job?"

"Yeah," Raymond said.

"Well, my name is Rick, and I've been told you'll get paid for cleaning up the parking lot here after the football crowd made a mess of everything last night."

Raymond rubbed his nose with the palm of his hand and replied simply, "Yeah."

The parking lot attendant led Raymond to the custodian's closet and introduced him to the various implements of cleaning.

"Here's the mop and bucket. Here's the outside broom and pan. Here is the wax and buffer machine. Up on the shelf are the cleaning sponges and paper towels and disinfectant. We also have a couple of reams of garbage bags and some odor spray. Do you think you can handle this?"

Raymond paused for a second because he wasn't sure what to say. He then carefully chose his words, "I think I can handle it." The parking lot attendant handed Raymond the closet keys and walked back to his post. Raymond stuffed the keys into his pocket and turned to enter the cleaning closet, unsure which implement to use first. He first reached for the outside broom but then decided he probably should tackle the garbage bags first because there probably was a lot to pick up in the parking lot.

He spent a lot of time picking up things in the parking lot that night, and he would look up from his work every so often to stare at the city's lights. The parking lot that he was working on was on a second level above the street, and he could hear the distant cars on their nightly sojourns to their unknown destinations.

* * *

Raymond Delosis remembered his time in the city when he would haunt the used record and bookstores in the area with friends. His friends were all part of the rebellious set in his high school. They would dye their hair purple or red or any other color they wished to. They listened to a lot of the alternative music that was sold in the record stores and were interested in the alternative comics that were sold in these stores.

He remembered walking with some of his friends with their rock band T-shirts and punk hairstyles down lighted streets at night when the stores closed, trying to find a place where they could assemble and meet for some kind of activity or fun. Sometimes, they would meet at a pizza place in the daytime and watch "the responsible ones" walking through town in their suits and ties or other business clothes going about their regular daytime activity.

SURVEYS AND SCAMS

They would think about their music and make recalcitrant remarks about authority and other "grown-up" friends that got on with their lives in the "adult" world. Raymond felt he never fit into any social set and was always searching for some kind of identity for himself.

He didn't have many close friends and usually met the only close friend he had at the pizza place in town. His name was Jack Breen, and he was a young man in his early twenties who talked with a stutter and was slightly balding for his age. He also had a lazy left eye and wore eyeglasses. Both had an interest in comics and frequently went to the comics store.

Raymond himself was a small, lithe person with dark hair that was short and stuck up in a punk style. He wore no glasses but usually knew how to dress well. He found the money to get designer jeans and nice shirts and usually wore the cheap sneakers that always were in style.

On this day, Raymond entered the pizza place and saw Jack sitting at one of the center tables drinking a shake and eating a slice. He patted Jack on the shoulder and sat down beside him. Jack gave an acknowledgment and continued to stare across the room at the window that showed the street outside.

"On a clear day like this, you can see all the way down the field to the houses in the distance. I watch people going in and out of them and sometimes can get involved in the games that are played by the kids in the field." Jack articulated this in a pleasant tone and resumed the eating of his pizza.

"I don't pay attention to passersby," Raymond muttered.

"You should," Jack replied.

Raymond wasn't sure if Jack really meant this comment or if he was just saying it out of turn. Jack then smiled and continued the commentary of his afternoon observations.

"I think the police are getting more emboldened in their rounds of the neighborhood," Jack said.

"They have to after that murder of a man by a drug dealer a month ago," Raymond mumbled. He talked in a very low tone that at the time wasn't always audible, and when he talked, he would not stare at the person he was speaking to in the eye. Jack was used to speaking to Raymond though and always understood what he said.

"Do you really think it's more dangerous here than it used to be?" Jack asked Raymond.

Raymond gave a wry smile as he knew Jack was a left-winged goon who always had a conspiracy theory up his sleeve.

"I don't think they are cracking down any more than usual, and I don't think they have an agenda to wipe us all out like you think."

Jack remained quiet as he digested what Raymond said the same way he digested the pizza he was eating. After a long moment of silence, he finally replied, "I'm not a conspiratoriologist, just a skeptic."

Raymond sat back and thought about that and replied, "I've noticed things about the police and the law, but my beef is more with society's norms and mores. Like if you think too independently or become too independent, you can be branded a criminal."

"It's all part of the master plan. They don't want us thinking independently. It's all in 1984 if you want to read it," Jack said.

"I don't like reading books," Raymond mumbled.

"Well, that's where your problem arises. If you're not informed of the way your society operates and aware of your own surroundings, you'll never know how you fit into your surroundings," Jack replied.

"That's too much for me to understand. I'm just learning how to be a custodian right now."

"You want the rest of my pizza?" Jack asked.

"Sure."

Jack got up and left Raymond to the pizza as the pizza owner was making his last rounds of serving pizza and shakes to his young clientele. Raymond made sure he ate the rest of the pizza and then filed out of place with the others.

Raymond didn't know what to think of Jack's suspicious meanderings. He decided the best thing to do was not to think. Thinking led to unsavory schemes and illicit plans. Thinking led to greater anger and resentment than what he already had. Thinking and speculation only led to paranoia and dementia, and he was not going to travel down that road.

He walked home that night, only thinking of his money situation and how to solve it. He had some kind of job now, but it never was enough to do all he would like to do. It was never enough to make him happy when he felt the need to make himself happy. It made him happy to buy a CD or DVD at a store or a pizza or arcade game at the pizza place. He still lived at home though and was subject to his parent's rules and authority which he would always have a beef with.

He came home to a small house with a normal wire fence around the yard to keep the Rottweiler in. He opened the gate and was met by sparkles. Sparkles didn't seem to have any emotion and didn't usually bark when Raymond came in. He was a very tame dog.

Raymond scratched sparkles head and walked into the small two-bedroom home of his parents. As was his usual behavior, he avoided eye contact and communication with his parents in the living room and, with stealth, ambled his way into his bedroom. At his door hung a poster of the punk band the Ramones. He entered the room and threw his jacket on the bed.

A small box of doughnuts was lying on the floor, and Raymond opened it to grab the last one. He liked to eat but remained a thin young man. A doctor had told him he had a high metabolism and was really not in any great threat of becoming overweight at this time. Raymond never worried about gaining weight as he always was doing something on the streets and was active all the time even though he was not a sports-minded person.

He turned his television on because there was a good zombie movie coming on that he wanted to watch. His television sat at the foot of his bed so that he could lay on the opposite end on his elbows and look directly into the television set. His mother was always telling him he was going to go blind that way, but Raymond ignored what he considered "parental picking." He ate his doughnut and soon became disinterested in the zombie movie and retired for the night.

When Raymond woke up the next morning, he knew he had to be at his gig at the parking garage as a custodian at noon. He had to walk there, so he would have to set off early to get there on time. He usually took two minor streets before traveling down to the main street that led into the city and the parking garage. He went into the kitchen and poured him a bowl of cereal and tried to work out the month's finances in his head as he was eating his cereal.

After gulping down his cereal in seven minutes, he realized he would be coming up a little bit short this month in his budget. He still owed a friend some money and had rent to pay to his parents. He went back to his room and sorted out the clothes he would wear that day. Being disorganized didn't always help, but he had some kind of organization in his chaos.

The morning wore on until he decided to leave early so he could get a head start on things. He could possibly meet another solitary friend of his who could have been considered a "frenemy." A lot of former friends of Raymond seemed to have become more like frenemies now. He remembered them being fairly good friends of his until they began to become more abusive to him as he grew to know them more. It seemed to always be that way with him for as long as he could remember.

As he was walking down one of the minor streets from his house, he passed one of his frenemies' houses. It was a little bigger than his was and, unlike theirs, had a living room that no one sat in. He noticed a third car in the driveway, and all of a sudden, Greg rolled out from under the car and turned to see Raymond.

"Hey, hey, Raymond."

Greg had light brown hair that almost looked blond and was almost a head taller than Raymond. He waved a wrench at Raymond, and Raymond lifted his head in acknowledgment.

"Come on over here, Raymond, and let's shoot the shit!"

Raymond reluctantly walked over to Greg's driveway and rubbed his nose and stood in a submissive stance next to Greg's car.

"So how's life treating you?" Greg said.

"I'm doing all right. I've got a job now."

"Yeah, but what kind of friends do you have now?"

"I've never been interested in having a whole lot of friends," Raymond said under his breath.

"Well, I've got all types of friends now. I'm in a fraternity," Greg replied.

"How do you know they're your friends?"

"I paid money to get into the fraternity, didn't I?" Greg said.

"Are you still going to the pizza place?"

"They've still got Defender, and the pizza is still good," Raymond said in a guarded way.

"My score is still the high score," Greg accentuated.

"Have you been in there recently?"

"I know no one can beat that score, so I don't go in there to check on it."

With that note, Raymond decided to part ways with Greg and stated, "I've got to get going to my job now."

He began to walk down Oakland and could hear Greg in the distance, saying, "Don't you want to hear about my fraternity and new sports friends?"

Raymond kept walking down Oakland until he made his turn at the second minor street called Jacob Street. He didn't know much about the people and houses in this area and decided to always keep a wide berth of the neighborhood. The people there were always overly concerned about the condition of their lawns and a "pride of ownership" with lawn mowers that had a sound that seemed to duplicate their pent-up anger and frustration.

It was when he got to the main road that led to the downtown parking garage that he saw on the side of the road what looked like some kind of card. He bent down and picked it up and noticed it was a credit card from a bank called Owners Bank. They were a bank he remembered seeing downtown near his place of work, and he read the name on the card: Susan Collins. He pocketed the card and kept walking down the main street. He wasn't sure what he was going to do with the credit card but wasn't going to think about that now. He had a job to go to.

He reached the parking garage, and lurking in the corner was one of the coworkers. He remembered him as being Rupert. Rupert tended to shirk work a lot and was always suggesting things to do apart from what needed to be done. He was always full of ideas and rambunctious nature. He looked up to see Raymond and made his way round the parking pole to give one of his usual off-the-cuff remarks to Raymond.

"You here for the usual bullshit work?"

"I've got to pay my debts up and save for some kind of transportation," Raymond replied.

"Well, I've done all I want to do for today," Rupert said. "It's your turn now." He handed the outside broom to Raymond.

"You know what I found on the road today?"

"A dead cat."

"This credit card." Raymond pulled out the credit card from his wallet and handed it to Rupert.

Rupert was immediately interested and turned it over and over in his hand. "Have you thought about using it?"

"That wouldn't be the honest thing to do," Raymond said.

"Yeah, but think of all the great things you could buy with it," Rupert said. "You know, all you have to do is push credit on those machines that you slide it with and sign it in a way where they can't tell the person's signature."

Raymond didn't trust everything Rupert said but, for some reason, still respected Rupert in various ways. They both liked the same movies and comic books. Rupert wasn't a picky eater like a lot of the other kids were. Raymond himself was a picky eater, which drove his mom and dad mad. For some reason though, he respected Rupert for that.

When he was finished with his cleanup work at the garage, he started to make his way home. Sometimes, his dad would pick him up if he was going that way, but Raymond didn't mind walking. He usually got himself something to eat at some vending machines at a local bus station nearby.

He was thinking about what Rupert had said about the credit card and would go into various stores, looking at the merchandise. The clerks in the stores were always standoffish and tucked their nose up at his hairdo. He thought about playing a trick on them. He threw the idea in the back of his mind when he got home.

He skipped out of his house that night to make his way to the pizza place and hopefully have a slice with Jack. He got there around about seven-ish and noticed Jack wasn't there as he usually was. He noticed the other kids from the more affluent neighborhoods were there with their friends. They always had the chance to play more video games and order more pizza. They also wore clothes that had some kind of status related to it. Some insignia or symbol was embossed on their shirts to give them the feeling of social status.

Raymond walked over to one of the video arcade games that one of the upper-class boys was playing and watched him play. The boy snapped at Raymond, "Stop staring over my shoulder. I need some elbow room."

Raymond was used to these rude remarks by these types of boys. They were the privileged ones, and privilege begets disrespect of others without the privilege. Raymond didn't let it bother him, although he couldn't help but feel a little offended. Instead, he went over to the grill and ordered him a pizza slice. He felt he would be on more equal footing with the cook and customers over there.

He took his pizza silently and walked to a checkered table. At times, he preferred to be alone and eat his slice. This was such a time. As he began to eat his pizza, he sat and stewed over his predicament. He thought about his life under the rules of his parents and how his job didn't give him the freedom to live on his own. He thought of how his frenemies seemed to go on with their somewhat successful lives achieving some kind of happiness while he was only left with his bottled-up emotions. Anger and resentment grew inside of him, and he decided to wash it down with a cold coke.

When he finished his pizza meal and coke, he slipped out of the pizza joint and began thinking about his newfound credit card. After careful thought, he decided to go to the local drugstore to buy some candy and magazines with the credit card.

Before entering the drugstore, he took his hoodie off of his head, thinking he would look less suspicious. After getting the candy and magazines, he did what Rupert told him he could do. For a brief minute, he was tense before the card reader at the cashier finally said that it was approved.

He walked out of the drugstore nonchalantly and made his way back home. He didn't get the feeling of pleasure and revenge that he thought he would have from this. All he felt was nervous and anxious. As he began to eat the candy though, he got a feeling of satisfaction that he had never felt before. When he was in his room, he began to look through the magazines, and the feeling of satisfaction continued.

That night, he went to bed with the magazine on his chest and didn't wake up until eleven o'clock the next day. He was a little groggy, but he wolfed down a bar of candy he had and made his way to the front porch of his house. He yawned and scratched his chest, thinking of what the next day will bring him by way of fortune.

He made his way to his job that day without incident. He entered the parking garage and noticed a larger amount of trash than usual strewn everywhere. The parking garage attendant stepped out of his office and stammered at Raymond, "It looks like you got your work cut out for you. I want you to get work on it ASAP. No complaint or smart-alecky remarks."

Raymond decided to be diligent in his work and did what his supervisor asked of him. He wasn't the nicest supervisor, but he knew he had to put up with it if he wanted to keep the job. While the supervisor was looking the other way, Raymond took out a Charleston chew and bit into it. He then started to pick up some of the debris and became more attuned to his work. He wished he was able to listen to his iPod, but it wasn't allowed on his job.

As he cleaned up the trash, he thought of who he was cleaning up after. He knew a majority of them were football revelers and possibly college frat kids on their mindless rampages. He heard of people known as "untouchables." They were a class or sect of society in India that worked in the salvaging and disposal of garbage and trash in India. No one in the higher and upper sects of society wanted to touch them or interact with them. He felt that this country had the same type of social class but never admitted it.

"Leave me alone now. I have paperwork to do," Raymond's boss retorted and retired to his cubicle in the garage. The light was dim in the cubicle, and it was a very small room, but Raymond could see it had a desk, a computer, and a coffee maker. He always had a stash of doughnuts that he was never willing to share with Raymond and the normal air of belligerence that came with the type of work he had to do. Raymond noticed bus drivers had a similar type of anger they held inside of themselves.

Raymond worked for a couple more hours at the parking garage and went to report to the cubicle to show his work results. The boss walked out and checked his work performance as he was required to do. "Well, I guess that will have to do but don't expect to get any kind of raise for it." Raymond walked out of the garage without comment and headed home.

As he walked down the main road, he noticed the record store he always passed by every evening. He had a phonograph at home that still worked, and he was not an avid collector of records, but it still was an interest of his. He decided to walk into the record store and look around. The store had its different sections: jazz, rock, techno, and so on. He looked through the techno section as that was a current kick of his and found two records that he was interested in. He knew he didn't have the money for them but thought about the credit card again.

He felt apprehension about taking out the credit card and looking at it in the store, so he decided to grab the records he wanted and go up to the clerk and pay with the credit card. He bought the three techno albums he wanted and slowly walked out of the store.

A feeling of guilt inched into his consciousness as he was walking down the side street to his home. He wondered how much longer he was going to be able to use the credit card. He would like to be able to get some good clothes at the local trendy clothes store but thought maybe he was wanting too much. In the distance, he saw the light of his parent's house and was thankful for them leaving it on for him.

He walked into his home and realized he had some pizza money left in his pizza money box under his bed. He took the cash and change out of the box and decided to go down to the pizza place.

He was hoping he was going to see Jack there and talk to him about things.

* * *

At the pizza place, Jack Breen was fidgeting with his backpack, thinking about the day's news on the television. He knew every news outlet had its angle, and he didn't take everything said at face value. Jack was skeptical about a lot of things, and at times, he was overly paranoid about the way his society was operating.

As Jack was contemplating the world, Raymond entered the parlor, and a relaxed smile came across Jack's face. He was happy to see Raymond and waved him over to the seat across from him.

Raymond took the seat but remained silent until Jack spoke. "How are you doing at your job, Raymond?"

"The boss is a jerk," Raymond replied. "But I'm able to do it with no problem."

"Most of them are jerks. Once in a while, you might find a nice boss," Jack said with a wink of reassurance.

"I thought I should go ahead and tell you I found this credit card on the road where I walked to work."

"And...?"

"I've already used it a couple of times at various stores, and I haven't run into any problems with the purchases."

A serious expression came over Jack's face. "You won't get away with it forever, Raymond."

"So far, so good," Raymond replied.

"These stores and policemen have all types of ways of catching petty thieves."

"I'll eventually ditch the credit card. There still are some clothes I want to get."

"Eventually, they'll find out. You know, they want the poor to remain poor. If a poor person gets a little more than they should, they get a little edgy about it," Jack explained. "It's February too."

"So what if it's February?"

"That's the month that the rich get the poor all tied up in court or in jail. They do this so they can have the freedom to go on their vacations in June," Jack said.

Raymond ignored what Jack said and ordered his pizza from the new waitress on duty. She was sort of a cute girl who tended to her own business. He thought of getting some new clothes from the boutique in town to impress her. He knew he was probably getting his hopes up for nothing, but having a girlfriend was on his mind sometimes.

Jack watched Raymond eyeing the waitress with a sly smile on his face. "You know you're asking for trouble getting to know a girl like that," Jack said.

Raymond gave Jack a distasteful smile and ate his pizza. He didn't like it when Jack poked fun at him.

"I'm sorry, Raymond. I'll try not to make your life miserable. It just seems that some people's lives are predetermined to turn out a certain way, whether they like it or not. I don't think you're an exception."

Jack finished his pizza and picked up his backpack. "Don't worry about it though, Raymond. There's a lot you can do to fight these problems. You've got a long life ahead of you that could be used for good purposes. I'll see you." Jack put his hand on Raymond's shoulder and walked out of the pizza parlor.

Raymond finished his pizza and looked around one last time at the people in the parlor. He paid at the counter and walked out.

* * *

Raymond walked into the boutique and began to look around at the various clothes on the hangars. He decided not to go hog wild at this place, so he picked out a couple of shirts and some jeans. He went to the cash register and purchased the items with a credit card. The cashier cashed in the items and handed the bagged merchandise to Raymond.

Raymond walked out of the store and walked home, which was only a few blocks away. It was nighttime when he was walking down the street, and he carried the bag over his shoulder, trying to get home as soon as he could. As he was panting on his walk, he heard behind him the bellowing of a police siren and saw illuminated on the sidewalk and street the various colors of a police car siren.

He looked behind him and saw the police car as it pulled beside him, and he heard the policeman say through the car's window, "Please stay right there by the sidewalk while I pull the car over to the side of the road."

Raymond waited while the policeman got out of the car and began to start asking Raymond the regular questions before incarceration. He ended the process by explaining to Raymond the charges. "You have been charged with fraudulent use of a credit card, and we will have to take you into custody at this time. Please step into the police car." Raymond entered the back seat of the police car and heard the gentle thud of the door being closed by the policeman.

As the light of the street lamps showed their trajectories into the police car, the policeman was driving Raymond to the station. Raymond looked out the window at the signs and storefronts, casting their glow and colored hues into the night. He couldn't help but think of what Jack said how it seemed to be already predetermined what was happening to him. He turned up his lapels on the old jacket he was wearing and prepared himself for the long journey home.

The White Supremacists League

I sat on the bus seat, looking at the town that was coming into view of my bus window. It was the town of Salt Springs, Utah, not easily seen on a map of the state. I traveled there because I wanted a place where I could be free from the hustle and bustle of the city and what I felt was a continuous cop problem in my state. My name is Derrick, and I lived for many years in the state of Illinois near Chicago. I've been "down by law" a couple of times there, and I felt a refreshing change from my former life which was what I needed.

I took the bag from the overhanging compartment when the bus driver announced over the intercom that we had reached the town of Salt Springs. I was surprised that there was actually a bus stop in this small town and was happy to get on my feet again. The few that were getting off at this stop grudgingly put their headsets up, stretched and yawned, scratched themselves, and began their procession through the bus aisle, down the steps, and into the bus stop at Salt Springs. I was happy to see a Waffle House next to the bus station and made my way there.

As I walked into the Waffle House, I saw a variety of nighthawks in the diner. It seemed loneliness was a way of life here as it was in the city. There was a couple in one booth, and I saw an empty booth next to them, so I took it. I sat in the booth for a while and then laid my arm over the top and spoke across it to the couple.

"Where can you find employment in this town?" I asked.

They looked at each other and laughed.

"This is not the town for employment of any kind," the woman said. "There is a temp agency down the street about a mile away." She pointed in an easterly direction. "It's called Temp World, and you can usually find a position in one of the manufacturing plants here in town."

"I wouldn't get my hopes up about a permanent position though," the man said. "That takes a lot of angling and sucking up."

"Are they closed now?" I asked.

"Yup. It's way too late. It gets dark here at about eight. They closed around five."

"Is there anything else I need to learn about this town?"

"Well, if you're White, you will probably do a whole lot better," the man said, and the woman affirmed with a laugh and a smile.

"What do you mean?" I said.

"There's a lot of businesses in this town controlled by White supremacists. All you've got to do is go into a bar, and you probably will talk to one," the man said.

"Are there any bars open tonight?" I said.

"Yes, there's one down the street called the Happy Man. They're open until two. I've been in there before. They've got all types of German beers," the man said.

"I think I might head on down there," I said as I walked out of the Waffle House. I looked back at their booth and saw the man raise his head as a farewell nod, and I did the same.

* * *

I came to the entrance and looked at the sign above. It showed a masculine male face smiling and holding a fist with a thumb in the upright position. I knew I was at the right place. The doorman looked me over and waved his hand for me to come in. I walked into the gloomy vestibule and saw through the windowed doors that the place was crowded. I heard the voices of the people in the next room and could hear the shouts and yelps of some of the women playing some of the bar games. I opened the windowed doors and made my way to the main bar.

A hazy light lit the bar and bartender, and I could see some of the German beers in the darkness behind him. I asked for a Pauli Girl, and the bartender gave me a scornful look as if I didn't make the right choice. I looked around at the other people in the bar and saw what I considered to be the regular bar fare—single men and women looking for time to kill on a weekday night, workers from various factories in the area getting their fill after a hard day's work, husbands coming in after work trying to find a way to unwind before heading home to their wives.

I slowly drank my beer, looking at the mainly White crowd of people before seeing a man at a table waving to me to join him. I walked over to the table with my Pauli Girl and sat in the chair across from him.

He was a burly man with a beard and eyeglasses, and he looked at me with a wry smile. He had a German beer that I had never heard of, and my immediate assumption was that he had a well-paying job for many years and was probably some kind of collector—maybe of rare toys or sports memorabilia or maybe German beer bottles.

"You don't seem to be around from these parts. Have you come to this town for a job, or are you down by law?" he said in a joking way.

"I've come here from Illinois to avoid the cops and crime."

The man looked at me with a distasteful expression. He paused and then made his comment, "You don't seem to fit in with the type of people that live in this area. You may not own up to the standards of this town."

I sat there for a while, not knowing what to say until I replied, "I think I have a lot to contribute to this town, and you would be doing this town a great disservice by not considering me." I realized what I was saying was telling him a load of bullshit—like something you would hear a public official say in a local newspaper—but I thought he would buy it.

"Son, do you think you can convince me with a crock of bull-shit like that?" he answered me. "Let me tell you what you need to do. You need to take the next bus out of here to a town that doesn't see through talk like that because this town is not that way."

"I've heard some comments about this town that it favors Whites. I feel the same way about this. I want to be in on this game." I made this comment to counter what he told me. It was a lie. I didn't want to be in on any kind of game but said it to try to get him to divulge some information.

The man inspected his fingernails and thought about what I said. He gave me a discerning look and replied, "There's a group here in town that pulls a lot of the strings in business and politics in the area. They meet secretly at designated places, usually on the outskirts of town. They call themselves the 'White Supremacists League.'"

"How do you get to be in an organization like that?" I asked.

"They let you into the secret meeting if you show a mark on your hand. You have to be initiated by the group in order to get the mark."

"How are you initiated?"

"It usually involves some kind of hazing ritual," the old man said.

"Is there a way to get into the secret meeting without the hazing ritual?"

"They might take a guest if they feel it's appropriate."

"How do you get to be a guest—"

The man held up his hand and said, "You're asking too many questions. I think I know where this is going, and I'll tell you right now it won't be that easy to enter a meeting as a guest."

I pushed a little too hard and knew it. I then tried a different strategy.

"What are the main interests of the town? What do people like to do around here besides drink?"

"There's a country club on a county road south of here. A lot of the big wigs hang out there. They play golf and have gambling games that are seasonal. If you get a job there, you might be able to find out more about the league."

I felt this was sufficient information to get from the old man and decided I would try for a job at the country club at Temp World the next day. I said goodbye to the old man and finished the last gulp of my drink. I knew I needed to find a motel room for the night, so I headed out to one that was three blocks away from the Happy Man.

*　*　*

I was in Temp World the next day, filling out an application, when I noticed someone sitting beside me with a child in the seat next to them. Small talk was not my specialty, but I decided to get into a conversation with her.

"Is this the first job agency you've been to?"

"Yes. There's another one in town, but I have heard they don't really have good-paying jobs. I have a kid to think about. Is this the first place you've been to?" she asked.

"Yep," I said.

We were silent for a while, not knowing what to say to each other until I broke the ice by asking a question about the town's restaurants.

"So what is the good places to eat around here?"

"I don't get to eat out that much, but when I do, I go to the fast foods here in town. I can't afford to leave tips."

She resumed her concentration on the application, and I was already finished with mine. It was then that the clerk called my name, and I went up to her desk. She motioned for me to sit in the chair, and as I sat down, she began to ask various questions that were commonly asked in a temp agency.

"Is there any certain job that you would like?" she asked.

"Is there an opening at the country club?" I asked.

"All we have are dishwashers. Would you like that?"

"I guess I'll take it," I said.

She explained to me where the place was and what day and time to report. I listened closely and took the job order card that was required of me to have at the job site and left the office. On my way back to the motel room, I thought about what the old man said about the league. He didn't seem to disclose a whole lot about the requirements of membership and getting into the secret meetings, but I felt I had some inside information that was helpful in finding out about the group.

I didn't know why I was gaining interest in this group, and I wasn't sure if I wanted to attend the secret meeting to infiltrate it or satisfy some kind of yearning to be in a group like this. I did have the basic requirement: I was White. I have been told though that I'm a goof-off, and my reason might be just for kicks. I think though I was doing it for curiosity's sake rather than getting any kind of jollies.

In the motel room, I noticed the local paper, *The Silver Springs Gazette*, was on my bed. I was aware of a lot of the small-town papers and the type of news they had—mainly dull articles about charity clubs and prominent people in the community getting awards. Every so often, an article about a crime in the area was described. I would find something like that interesting to read. After scanning it briefly, I saw nothing interesting and decided to ditch it.

The next day, I was up bright and early to go to the place of work that was listed on my work order card. It was a long walk, but it was a nice day, and it really wasn't too far away. As I was walking down the county road, someone stopped and offered a ride. I said "sure" and got in.

The driver was a short, stocky guy from what I could tell, and he was bearded like a lot of these men were. The country club was just five miles ahead, so we only had a few interchanges to make. I mentioned I had a job opportunity at the country club, and when we arrived, he said, "I wish you the best of luck, but you're really pushing your luck here."

I tried to say something to him like, "What do you mean by that?" but he had already pulled out of the parking lot.

I went to the front desk and showed the lady at the desk my work order card, and she looked at it and smiled and said, "Two doors down the hall to the left is the kitchen staff. You'll meet your boss there."

I walked down the hallway and entered the kitchen, where the staff congregated. An office to the side had a man sitting at a desk, filling out some paperwork that I assumed was my employer.

"My name is Derrick, and I am here from Temp World," I said.

"You're exactly who I am looking for," the man said in a gruff voice. He was shorter than me with a little more weight on him, but this man was clean-shaven. "Let me have your work order card, and I will get you started."

I handed him the work order card, and he wrote something on it and directed me to the kitchen.

"We'll have you on the dishwashing staff for most of the day. There are big steak dinners being served tonight for our clientele here. They're all golfaholics and are entitled to a steak dinner when they are finished. You can talk to Betty for any directions and questions you might have about your job."

I entered the kitchen and saw two or three workers in the dishwashing room but didn't see Betty, so I decided to go ahead and put on the aprons that were hanging on the wall near the pile of dishes. Maybe it would impress them if they saw a worker take the initiative. At the dishwasher, I began loading dishes, not paying much attention to the other worker beside me. Soon after about ten minutes of silence, we began to chat. He had a small and thin build and was bearded with fairly long hair.

"Are you new here in town?" he asked.

"Just arrived two days ago," I said.

"Well, my name is Darren, and I've lived here all my life, so any questions you have about this town you could probably ask me."

I thought about what he said and decided to immediately cut to the chase. "Actually, I was wondering about a White supremacist's group here in town and where they held their secret meetings."

He answered with a nontransparent look about him as if he wasn't fazed by what I said at all and answered, "I could fill you in about them. I don't personally go to the meetings, but I could set up or arrange a meeting with one of the members. A couple of big wigs in this town run the group and the meetings, and my own dad is a member. He and I had a falling out about it. Do you want to know about it out of curiosity or what?"

"I've always been interested in secret societies and such," I lied to him.

"Well, the league meets every first Wednesday somewhere in the town limits, usually on someone's private property," Darren said.

"Isn't there some kind of mark you have to show in order to get into the meetings?"

"I have a friend who I can arrange to meet with you and give you a mark if you want one."

I paused and thought about this. I was a little hesitant and afraid to accept his offer, but always being somewhat of an adrenaline-junky, I went ahead and gave my response.

"That sounds all right."

"Well, then listen closely because I can't let anyone know about what I am telling you," Darren began to whisper.

"I'll arrange it where you can meet Damon outside the town library on the benches where a lot of library-loiterers hang out. Give me your number, and I'll call you about the day and time."

I wrote the number down and handed it to him, and he responded with a slap on the shoulder.

"I'll take care of it," he said.

* * *

It was in the Happy Man that I waited for Darren's contact to meet me. He gave me the time and place to meet him, but he seemed to be a little late. I sat at a back room table and imagined these types of guys are always late for a clandestine meeting like this.

I was eating my order of chicken wings when I saw a short, stocky man enter the back room. He looked around, and I waved to him. He acknowledged my greeting and sat down in a booth next to mine. He put his arm on the booth next to mine and began to talk to me.

"You're Derrick?"

I replied with a yes.

"Well, I have the handstamp equipment in my car. I was thinking we could do this in the bathroom. It would be the most discreet way of doing things. I don't want anyone in the Happy Man to see what we're doing. It's just common practice for the White

Supremacists League to do things this way. I hope you don't mind. My name is Damon."

He reached over the booth and shook my hand.

Damon then head-motioned me, and I followed behind him as we walked across the back room to the bathroom. We opened the door that said gentlemen on it and walked up to a sink with a mirror. Damon looked around to make sure the place was unoccupied and grabbed my hand as he took out the marking kit. He made a stamp on my hand and then quickly put the stamper and pad back into the large pocket of his jacket.

We walked out of the door, and Damon made his last gesture to me with a nod of his head and said, "I hope you learn something from the next meeting at the barn near the landfill. From what I heard, one of the big-wig community leaders will be there to conduct the session. Good luck."

As he walked off, I stared at my hand. The sign was in red ink and seemed to be some kind of insignia with a red skull on the top portion. The bottom portion was shaped sort of like an ankh. I hoped this was going to get me into the meeting without any problems, and I hurried off into the night. I was going to try to get some sleep for the next couple of days and for my work at the country club.

The night I received the phone call, I had almost given up on Darren's tip-off to the secret meeting. He told me it was the first Wednesday of the new month, and it was being held in a prominent farmer's barn near the county lake. He told me it was customary for guests to bring a flashlight. I told him I could get one with no problem. He proceeded then to give me directions to the barn, and I made sure to write it down. He wished me good luck and hung up.

That night, I went to the convenience store and bought the flashlight. While I was in the convenience store, I couldn't help but be a little paranoid of the other customers in the store. I wondered if they knew about the league or if they possibly knew what I knew. I walked back to the hotel room, thinking about transportation to the secret meeting, when I came to the conclusion that I would take a taxi to some outpost near the barn and walk the rest of the way there.

* * *

The night of the secret meeting was just a week away, and I wondered about the mark on my hand and various other things. The mark didn't seem to fade and kept its color. It must have been some kind of paint, but I knew nothing more of Damon's mark-making kit. I wondered if Damon would be there himself but then quickly erased such ramblings from my mind.

The night of the meeting, I had the cab drop me off at a convenience store one mile away from the barn. The convenience store had a greyhound bus stop outside, and I decided to wait at the bench there. The day was warm, and it was just before evening as I apprehensively looked at my watch, waiting for the moment to make the walk to the barn.

I decided to give myself an hour before I made my walk on the county road that Darren told me to take. I was glad the convenience store was an all-night one so that I could call for a cab on the way home. As I looked at the horizon, it was red from the falling sun, so I decided to make my trek. I wanted to have enough light on my way there.

As I was walking down the county road, I noticed various cars and trucks would pass me on the road with loud country or rock music playing out their windows. I would also hear raucous laughter and shouting from the windows as they passed by. It was beginning to get dark when I saw the conflagration of cars and trucks on the lot that I assumed was where the meeting was. Music was playing, and I could hear shouts and loud talking as I saw the wooden mailbox with the number that Darren told me was the mailing address. Flashlights were beaming everywhere, and some faggots were lighted and placed in what looked like the barn loft. I surmised these were lit by some of the senior members of the league. I walked onto the grassy field that surrounded the barn, wondering how they would check on marks but realized the meeting was going to take place in the barn.

I looked around at some of the young men and noticed a lot of them were very thin and shirtless. Some of them had war paint on their faces and chests. Others wore the regular farmer's garb that was common to this area.

I noticed what seemed to be a line forming next to the barn and leading to a small side door. Other burly men were guarding the two big doors with their arms crossed. I decided to get into line for what I assumed was the checking of the hand marks. After a while, the line began to move, and I made it my priority to remain aloof from the other members of the line.

When I got to the door, the man at the entrance asked for my hand, and I showed him the mark. He beckoned me into the barn, and I followed the others inside. Lighted torches were all around the inside, and there was a large bandstand in the middle. Bales of hay were set up in uniform patterns throughout the barn, and men were already seated on some of them.

On the bandstand were a microphone and stand. Large speakers were also on either side of the bandstand, and I imagined they were used for possible musical performances in the area. As the members began to settle in the sitting spots provided by the bales of hay, I noticed various men assembling on the bandstand. A tall well-mannered man of middle age was talking to another short, burly bald man with what seemed to be a similar age.

The tall man tapped the microphone, and the talking died down very quickly. A high-pitched noise was heard, and then a lull in the crowd's activity signaled the beginning of the meeting. The tall man began to speak to the crowd the secret meeting's introductory speech.

"Well, I have you assembled here to talk about the growing problem in our society that is affecting us all. It involves the black encroachment into the idyllic society of the White. It has been happening for many years now, and unfortunately, we all have had our share of experiences we would probably like to discuss. For example, we are here not to just discuss Black behavior but homosexuality as well. If you have ever been in social circles with homosexuals and felt an uncomfortable feeling or annoyance around them, then you know what I am talking about. Has anyone any examples of what I mean?"

A man raised his hand, and the tall speaker pointed to him.

"I was in a place with friends when a homosexual threatened to kick my ass. I guess he was just joking, but I still felt offended by it. I wanted to say something to him but was too afraid of the repercussions I might get by what I might say."

"I'm sure a lot of you have been physically threatened by Black men as well," the tall speaker said. "Now I am the owner of the country club here in town, and I have had Black men as golf-caddies but nothing more than that. We can't have Black men taking control of high positions here, or they will gain too much of a foothold in this town. You know what will happen then. They'll start getting all our White women. I don't know about you, but I want to have sex with a White woman."

The audience gave yells and cries in agreement and raised their fists in jubilant excitement at the country club's owner's words. He gave an urbane smile and continued his speech.

"Having sex with a White woman is something all of us look forward to, and remember what Machiavelli said, 'Fortune is a woman.'"

He paused for a second and decided to change his thought.

"And that is what I worry about in this dawning age of miracles. The Black man has not gained a proper enough education but only one from a public school. Does he learn about Machiavelli, Lord Byron, Homer, Aeschylus, not to mention the great poets of our age such as Eliot and Frost?"

The crowd looked quizzical from the tall man's comments, but he ignored their reactions and kept talking.

"Now I know you don't have the level of sophistication that I have, but I want you to think about the things I've said and understand the purpose of the league. We're here to enforce the values and traditions of White folk, not to muddy the water with new ideals of nondiscrimination and social justice and equality. Keep that in mind as I pass the podium to Jeremiah."

He placed the microphone stand in front of the short bald man and sat down in a chair behind him. The husky bald man known as Jeremiah tottered back and forth on his heels, conveying a masculine image to the men in the barn. He smiled as he looked down before gathering his thoughts for the crowd.

"I'm here to talk to you about the growing need for the league. We need the manpower and energy that you men possess in abundance. You are the driving force and determination of the White folks' ideals and ambitions. Have you considered for a second all of what the Black man does to propagate his kind? They use brute and physical force as a career to advance themselves, those football and basketball athletes, as well as the sports of boxing and street fighting. They dominate the sport, and it's how they earn their money."

The crowd yelled in response to Jeremiah's accusations, and I couldn't help but be amused by what was going on. I was a little frightened by the whole affair and the look of the barn though and tried to keep my anonymity. I was still interested in hearing what Jeremiah had to say.

"As my mother used to tell me, they don't live like we do. They also are known to eat from the same plate. What I noticed most about them is a thing that I call Black Brainwashing. This is where they brainwash you into thinking that you can't have sex with a White woman. It happened to me when I was young and in the army, and I shared a hotel room with a Black man."

"This Black man was a womanizer who knew all the right lines and hygienic habits to get a White woman into his hotel room. He told me straight out that I would never be able to do what he did in the hotel room we had together. I had another Black man that told me after I had a mix-up with a woman that it would be best if I stayed away from women. They want to make it understood in your mind that you have no business interacting with a White woman."

The crowd gave their typical shouts and yells in affirmation of Jeremiah's words. I decided to join in on some of the yellings just to remain inconspicuous. As I was shouting, I felt a tap on my shoulder. I turned around and saw Damon looking at me. He leaned over and shouted in my ear, "It might be a good time for you to leave."

I didn't know what he meant by this. Was he asking me to leave because of the danger I would be facing from the league, or maybe was there some other kind of danger? I took his suggestion and started to walk out of my row of revelers and started to make it to the side door.

Just then, on the stage, Jeremiah was approached by another man who whispered something in his ear. Jeremiah took the mike immediately after that and shouted to the audience, "Unfortunately, fellow league members, our meeting has been revealed to the local police, and the sheriff is Black!"

The place was pandemonium as flashlights were beaming in all directions, and people were running for the exit. I managed to make it to the outside before being stampeded or squashed by anyone else. Once I was outside the barn, I decided to remain stationary as everyone else was running for their trucks. In the distance, I could hear the sirens begin to wail. As I was slowly making my way off of the property, Damon appeared out of the darkness.

"I can give you a ride home if you need it."

I followed him to the car, and we both drove off of the property.

"They seemed to be quick to run off from the cops," I commented as I watched the chaos of trucks and flashlights and police sirens disappear into the distance.

"Oh, this isn't the end of the league. They will probably reassemble in another place soon enough," Damon said.

"Who was the tall man that started the meeting?" I asked. "He didn't give his name."

"That's Robert Wentworth. That's Darren's dad."

"The one at the country club who set me up with you?"

"He had a falling out with his dad about the league and since then looks for people to help infiltrate the league. He may not inherit his dad's country club."

"So his dad knows about what he is doing?"

"Probably."

"It all sounds like a game," I said as the trees of the county road passed by me. Damon was silent from this, but I detected a suppressed feeling of frustration from his reaction. He seemed to keep a lot of the league's opinions to himself.

"Why do you go along with Darren if he is so against the league?" I asked Damon.

"I just try to recruit as many into the league as I can, and like you said, it's all a big game anyway," he replied and then looked down on the floor and said, "Besides, I could have a change of heart."

When we got to the motel, I stepped out of the car, and Damon said to me, "I probably won't be able to help you with any of the dealings of the league anymore." With that, he drove off. I wasn't confident that I might see him again, but I felt I might gain a friendship with Darren when I returned to the country club Monday morning.

Survey Today, Scam Tomorrow

The Dollar Saver sign came into view as Lalise drove her '92 Subaru into the parking lot of the shopping center that was situated somewhere between a residential district of the city she lived in and a very large shopping mall. She tried to avoid the shopping mall as much as she could because she couldn't afford the high-profile shops and boutiques there. The restaurants were too expensive too. She was glad that she passed the online honesty test and felt she was finally given some kind of opportunity for a job.

She got out of her car and walked through the back door of the Dollar Saver into the stockroom. Cluttered throughout the room were boxes of snack foods, underwear, as well as price guns, and other tools of the trade. She checked in at the computer and waited around the back room for a little while, hoping she could catch a conversation with one of the other employees that worked there.

She was about to give up hope when in walked another girl that had worked there for a while.

"Have you got the front register tonight?" Lalise asked Stephanie.

"No, I think I got the back tonight doing stockwork," Stephanie said.

Stephanie held back any comments she wanted to make about her backroom job for the night. She knew she was important for the store in various ways and didn't want to be the one who "rocked the boat." She realized Lalise was different and had a strong mind of her own, so she left such deliberations of the store's policies to her.

"I think I'm going to start stocking now," Stephanie said and made her way back to the stockroom.

Stephanie was a girl with a light complexion and riveting blue eyes. She had light brown hair and round facial features that belied her youth. She was a girl of anglic descent and felt she had a good chance in this company because of this.

Lalise, on the other hand, was of a dark complexion with brown eyes and black hair. She had a cute, round face and was also of a youthful age like Stephanie. Unlike Stephanie, she had a suspicious nature but tried to keep these thoughts to herself. Her mother had warned her not to be too much of a paranoiac. Lalise couldn't help sometimes but think of these things. She did well on the honesty test but knew things could be entirely different when you worked at a place.

That night, she ate dinner with her mother, thinking about her new job. Her mother was glad she found work and decided to celebrate with a fast-food meal of burgers and fries. Her mother had a job at a grocery store and was usually very tired at the end of the day.

"So do you think you'll like your new job?" her mother asked.

"Mom, you don't have to ask a dull, motherly question like that. You can ask something that you would really like to ask me."

"Well, then, do you think you're going to be treated fairly at your job?" her mother asked.

"I imagine so. I'm not going to worry about it on my first day, y' know?"

"Well, let's just eat our meal and be glad you found something."

Lalise looked across the dinner table at the stack of mail they got that day. She didn't have to scan through it to know what kind of mail it was. It was from organizations with their political surveys that they wanted you to fill out and a whole lot of scam mail of free trips to the Bahamas and work-at-home offers.

"All we seem to get are surveys to fill out and scams and frauds to try to cheat us out of a little money that we might have," Lalise said.

"Well, honey, you shouldn't have gotten into these things in the first place. They have your name now probably on a number of telemarketing lists, and that's why you're getting so much junk mail."

"Junk! Junk! That's all people want anymore in their houses. They want to fill their houses up with nothing but junk. The only mail you get anymore is junk mail. Nothing important. Nothing that can really help you," Lalise exclaimed.

"Things will change when you work. You'll see."

Lalise liked how her mother could calm her down and keep a positive attitude about things. She encouraged her to go out and get the job, and Lalise was happy when she passed the honesty test. She wondered though how truthful people were in answering questions on that honesty test. You could very easily fool people by making them think you were honest when you weren't.

* * *

Lalise came through the stockroom door located at the back of the store, hoping she could spend some time before her shift talking off the record with some of the other employees. She wanted to learn more about the honesty test and how the others answered a lot of the questions. As she walked through the door, a young employee named Nate looked up from his work on the pricing of items with a price gun at Lalise. He reacted with an eager, surprised look on his face and exclaimed, "Hey, girl!"

Lalise smiled and replied, "Hey, guy!"

Lalise knew enough about Nate to feel comfortable around him. He was an innocent, naive boy who was very enthusiastic about his work. He stayed out of other people's business and seemed to be smart in that respect. She didn't try to dissuade him from any of the viewpoints he might have about his work and the store. She was smart in that respect.

"Well, labor day is coming up, and we all still have to work," Nate joked.

"If we were government employees, we would get the day off," Lalise replied.

"I think that's good that a government employee gets the day off," Nate said.

"I didn't like it when I was expecting mail and wouldn't get it because of a holiday," Lalise said.

"You've got to think of the hard work they're doing and the fact that they need a break like that," Nate said.

Lalise nodded and walked out of the stockroom into the main store.

Dollar Saver was a store that sold mainly household incidentals such as toilet paper, toothpaste, cosmetic items, and a variety of canned foods and snacks. They would have stuff come on pallets from places they didn't know too much about, and the store would place these things on clearance to get them off the shelves and out of the store. Lalise wasn't sure what kind of deals the store was making with the unknown pallets of products that came through the stockroom, but that was a lot of the reasons why customers came to this store. They wanted to see the unique products that were sold in the store.

Lalise had only worked in the store a year, and Nate was only a month-old employee. Stephanie had been there about half a year and seemed to have a hard time adapting to the store's environment. She routinely made mistakes as the cashier, but the head manager seemed to want to overlook such things.

This brought her to her opinion of the head manager. His name was Bill Smith, a man in his early fifties who didn't seem to adhere to all the policies and regulations of the store. He seemed to have his own ideas on how Dollar Saver was to be managed. He had brown hair and blue eyes with handsome features and a slightly overweight and unkempt appearance. He kept a reading glass case in his shirt pocket and liked to hunt and fish. He supposedly had a large collection of guns in his home.

She heard his family had a very long line that went back to the founding of the nation. She would hear him brag about his heritage at times when another male manager from a nearby Dollar Saver came to discuss business. Lalise never had a high opinion of people with guns. Her mother had never owned one, and she always told her that they're "more trouble than what they are worth."

In the main store, Lalise saw Stephanie at the cash register and thought she might need some help. Stephanie managed to get the change for the current customer and turned to see Lalise. She waved and smiled at Lalise as she finished counting the change.

"This is not the correct change!" the customer said.

"Awwww," Stephanie answered with her usual insincere sympathy.

"She needs $50 back," Lalise said.

Stephanie counted the change and gave it to the customer.

"Sorry," she said.

Stephanie waited for the customer to leave before she turned on Lalise.

"You shouldn't have corrected me like that," she said acidly.

"I was just trying to help," Lalise said with subdued laughter.

Stephanie's shift was almost over, so Lalise decided to hang around and talk a little before her shift started.

"What have you heard about our weekly profits?" Lalise asked Stephanie.

"You know I don't keep track of things like that," Stephanie said.

"Well, I don't either, but I thought it might be good to know about that. You know, I've heard that gas stations don't even make their money from their gas. They make money from drawing people into their store to buy things like cigarettes and beer."

"They must make more money than that," Stephanie said.

"I don't know. That's just what I've heard," Lalise said.

"I don't know what Bill would think about this. I might ask him sometime," Stephanie replied.

Lalise was silent. She wondered what Stephanie's relationship with Bill was all about. Was he overlooking her incompetency on the job for a reason? She realized Stephanie was a pretty girl and had all the mannerisms and social clichés of a party girl down to a tee.

Lalise mustered up the courage and asked, "When do you usually talk to Bill?"

"He's invited me to some of his grill parties at his house. I talk to him about things there. We're usually pretty good friends."

Lalise wondered what she meant by "friends" but decided not to pursue it at this time. She decided to make her way back to the stockroom and get ready for her shift at the cash register. She was a little hungry, so she went into the little breakroom, hoping to find her snacks. She opened the fridge and saw that both of her homemade cupcakes were still there. She picked one and began to eat it when Nate came in.

"Can I have a cupcake?" Nate asked.

"Sure."

"You know I don't understand all the whining that goes on among certain types of people about how things go in this country," Nate said while eating the cupcake.

Oh, boy, he's going to go on about politics again, Lalise thought.

"You think they would be happy with what they've gotten and stop complaining," Nate said.

"Well, there are sheltered, protected people of privilege who don't know the real world, Nate," Lalise decided to say.

"I don't feel that I'm that way. I plan on enlisting in the army," Nate replied.

"Well, maybe you'll learn a whole lot more of life and understand other people's grievances more," Lalise said.

"I think it will make me more tough and better to handle life's problems and less of a whiner," Nate said.

"Maybe so," Lalise replied.

* * *

Lalise lay on her bed that night, waiting for her mother to come home from the second shift. She knew a little of what her mother's politics were as she was always complaining of no unions where they lived. She always said this is a "no-union town."

She heard the back door to their apartment open, and she knew it was her mother.

"Lalise, are you there?"

"I'm in the bedroom, Mom."

Her mother appeared at the door of Lalise's bedroom, looking in with a frown on her face.

"Come into the dining room. We haven't talked in a while," her mother said.

Lalise got up from her bed and walked into their little dining room. It was just a small table with four chairs but sufficient for their needs.

"Have you read any good books lately?" her mother said.

"I never know what to read. I went into a bookstore and looked around but got totally lost. I had no idea what to pick up."

"The schools give you ideas of what to read, but you eventually have to find something that sparks your own individual interest."

"I'm sort of interested in the politics that goes around these days," Lalise said.

"There's no way you can convince some people about their opinions on politics. They keep their opinion and don't want to hear any other opposing one."

"It seems to me a lot of people want to believe in their economic theories because it makes them feel above their station in life when they preach about it to others. Like if a poor person believes in capitalism, they feel good about themselves when they can explain an unknown economic theory to someone they've learned in a book that makes them appear smarter in the debate. They have the phony idea that they're 'above' others even though their station in life doesn't reflect that."

"People can be brainwashed to the point where they're totally blind to everything going on around them and even to what is directly happening to themselves," Lalise's mother said.

Lalise thought about that for a while and decided to change the subject.

"Are you glad you're getting third shift now?"

"I don't know how long it will last, but I'm glad I'm getting the third shift."

Lalise wondered why her mother always seemed to have gotten third shift for such a long time at the company. She couldn't help but feel like some kind of second-class citizen. She wondered why others got the first and second shifts while her mother had to work the night for so long. She supposed seniority had a lot to do with it, but she suspected other things.

Lalise sat at the dining room table with her head in her hands. Sometimes, she would get moods where she felt defeated by everything that was happening to her.

Her mother noticed this. "Are you doing all right, Lalise? You seem a little down," her mother said while putting her hand on her head and stroking her hair.

"Having to work a lot like this is not easy. I'm not used to it," Lalise said.

"Life can be tough sometimes. I don't like getting up every day and going to work. Somedays, I feel like lying in bed and not going to work, but once I'm on my feet and moving around, I feel better. Work won't hurt cha."

Lalise smiled and took her head out of her hands and hugged her mom.

That night, they had burritos and leftovers and talked about movies and movie stars they had seen. Lalise knew she couldn't really talk about music stars with her mother too much. It was definitely more of a "generational" thing. She was happy she and her mom had similar interests in movies though.

They talked the rest of the evening until they decided they were too sacked to talk anymore. Lalise retired to her comforter and bed while her mother went to her queen and called it a night.

* * *

Lalise was in the stockroom the next day with Nate, trying to unpack the new arrivals when Bill Smith entered.

"What's going on?" Lalise said.

"You!" Bill Smith pointed his two index fingers at Lalise. "I need to talk with you about some things. Come with me."

She followed him into his office, and he motioned to her, "Have a seat."

Lalise sat and waited while Bill Smith looked over his papers with his reading glasses and cleared his throat a few times in anticipation of his conversation with Lalise. Lalise didn't feel very comfortable in her chair waiting for his impromptu interview.

Bill Smith looked up from his desk and began talking.

"What do you know about the recent depreciation of our store's stock?"

"I'm not aware of it at all," Lalise said.

"Well, there's talk you and Nate had something to do with it."

"Me and Nate just do our job unpacking stock and pricing it," Lalise said.

"Well, there's talk you're doing more than this."

"Who's been telling you this?" Lalise said.

"I've heard it from a third-party source," Bill Smith said.

"Stephanie?" said Lalise.

"Well, yes, as a matter of fact, it was Stephanie."

"I don't feel Stephanie can be trusted in anything she says," Lalise said.

"Well, she does have a good relationship with the store manager."

"I do too, but I don't go around accusing people of things," Lalise said.

"Now, Lalise, we're not going to get anything started here with Stephanie. She is a valued member of the store," Bill Smith said.

"Me and Nate just take stock and price things. We don't steal from the store."

"Well, I am very busy and can't look into all this. I haven't decided yet whether to take any action on this matter. I might just leave it up for the store manager to settle. Good luck on your future prospects."

With that, Bill Smith left the room and walked out of the store to his truck. She knew he was one of those guys with a truck because that seemed to be a symbol of status where she lived. She always hated how those trucks blocked your view when you would try to pull out of a parking space. She could hear him whistling in the distance as she walked out of the office.

She decided when she had the chance, she would confront Stephanie about the accusations. She wasn't sure yet if she wanted to talk to the store manager about it yet. The store manager was a middle-aged woman that seemed to remain aloof of the store's problems.

Lalise knew that Stephanie was coming to work on a later shift that night, and she decided then was the time to confront her about the accusation. She wasn't sure quite yet what she was going to say to her, but she decided she was going to suck it in and gather up the courage to deal with this problem.

She went back to the storeroom where Nate was and began to have a conversation with Nate about it. As the conversation wore on, Nate began to make contentious comments about the whole affair.

"I don't believe we're being accused of something like this. I'm not used to things like this."

Lalise was thinking that there could be something happening with Stephanie and the store manager, that they might be the ones involved in the store's depreciation of stock. She knew she had a suspicious nature but felt these false accusations were cause for alarm.

Her conversation with Nate ended when Nate had to do his stocking of shelves at the front of the store. She walked around the stockroom, pondering her fate, when she was suddenly struck with an idea. The man that delivered the stock to the store seemed to be an honest and trustworthy person and had a delivery to make to the store in about an hour.

Lalise decided to wait in the stockroom until the delivery man came with the stock. She waited by the door, apprehensively worrying about what was happening to her. She wasn't afraid but couldn't help but harbor some anger and resentment about it all. She knew she had to control her impulses and bad feelings if she was to effectively communicate with the delivery man.

Within an hour, the delivery truck showed up at the back door, and the man showed up at the door with the packages. He came to the door, and Lalise opened it for him, hoping to get into communication with him at that time.

"Are you able to handle the deliveries all right today?"

"As well as I can," he said.

"They should give you double for what you do," Lalise chided.

"I know it," said the delivery man.

"I was hoping I could speak with you about something that might be going on in the stockroom when I'm gone."

"I think I might know what you're talking about," the delivery man said.

"Like what?"

"I overheard them talking about you, and it didn't seem to be too nice what they were saying."

"Was it Stephanie and the store manager Janice?" Lalise asked.

"That was the two, yes."

"What exactly were they saying?"

"They were saying things like they wanted to 'tag' this all on you. I also heard the store manager say that 'no one is going to miss this stuff if we just keep quiet.'"

"The regional manager has talked to me about missing stock and how I am being blamed for it," Lalise said.

"Well, if you need me for anything, let me know. I'll continue to do these deliveries to the store, and you can call my number here. My name is Roger."

He handed her his business card and walked out.

Lalise fingered the business card and then put it in her pocket and walked back to the front of the store. She felt she shouldn't waste too much time in the stockroom, and no one in front had missed her for that short period of time. She felt a little relief that she had someone on her side and felt confident of getting behind the cashier's counter.

* * *

The next day, Lalise knew that Stephanie would be in the stockroom with Nate and felt that she might have someone else on her side when she confronted her about the problem. She walked in through the front door and started to make her way back to the stockroom. She could hear Stephanie's laughter coming from the stockroom and knew she had to make her move.

"Hello, Stephanie," Lalise said.

"Well, hey, Lalise, how are you?" Lalise said with her usual false enthusiasm.

"Fair to middlin'," Lalise replied.

"Bill Smith talked to me about stock depreciation at this store and how I'm the one being blamed for it," Lalise continued.

"Well, you would seem like the type of person that would get into shenanigans like that. Right, Nate?" Stephanie said.

Nate was silent.

"You think you can blame me for a wrong? You need to think again," Lalise said with glowing eyes of fire.

"What pray tell can you do about it?" Stephanie said.

"I have a witness to you and the store manager's funny business," Lalise said.

"You think that is going to help you?" said Stephanie.

"I don't think I will have a problem explaining my case," Lalise said in what was somewhat of a bluff.

Stephanie was silent and looked over at Nate.

Nate finally spoke.

"I think you need to come clean."

* * *

It had been two weeks since Lalise had her confrontation with Stephanie, and she still had her job. The last she had heard, Stephanie had been transferred up to the regional offices where Bill Smith worked. The store manager though was going to be replaced by someone else from what Nate had told her.

She sat at her mother's table watching the television. It was the same old sitcoms and dramas that were always on. As she watched, she heard the mailman drop off the mail in the mailbox. She went to the door and opened it and took the mail, saying to the mailman, "Same old stuff?"

The mailman nodded. As she looked at the mail, she realized it was the day's regular collection of surveys and scams.

Videohead

The pixels on the video screen began to form an image for Rodney to watch as his eyes lit up in anticipation of the video game he was about to play. He ate his chips and thought about the current game's objectives and was uncertain how he was going to reach them as he was uncertain about a lot of things going on in his life. He never watched the news and knew little of what was going on in the world and government. He never had any friends or girlfriends to discuss his problems with and was a ward of the state. He was entirely dependent on the government.

The pixels once again disrupted the screen because of the rainy weather outside that Rodney was totally unaware of. He fingered the last chip in his bag and gave out a belch as the images on the screen finally came into focus. Rodney was playing the super Jenkins Bros, which was streamed onto his TV monitor that he pirated from his neighbor. He recalled vaguely how he was able to do this, but his cognitive skills were beginning to fade as his interest in video games increased.

He ate his chips and began to wonder about the rainfall outside. He knew the rainfall was a problem in this area but knew it was best not to worry about whether or not he was on a flood plain. He had more pressing concerns.

He was ensconced in his chair, trying to ignore the newsfeeds and amber alerts he was getting on his smartphone when he received a ringtone on his smartphone. It was a car warranty service that offered a plan at an inflated price. Unable to do the math in his head, he decided to take the deal from the representative.

He hung up and continued his video game excursions. He needed just one thousand points to beat his former score and knew he could do it by equipping one of the Jenkins Bros with a shotgun and a hunting knife. He took a chip from the bag on his snack table and coughed on it while he maneuvered the Jenkins Bros into position. He fired off the shotgun and made his winning kill.

Rodney was not as proficient at video games as some of his friends were, but he was beginning to pick up on some of their tricks. Learning the tricks of the trade was a way to win at the conventions they held every year. The cash payouts were sometimes big enough to live on for a couple of years. He knew if he kept up the training, he might start winning the tournaments. He only wished he understood the news more. He decided to give up watching it some time back.

A knock on his door caused him to throw down his control pad and walk up to the door. He brushed the door's drapes back and looked through the window at Abraham, a video friend of his. Abraham looked through the window at Rodney with a blank and docile look on his face. Abraham wore long hair and was a thin person like Rodney, but unlike Rodney, he was shy.

Rodney smiled and let Abraham in. Abraham came in slowly and looked around the room with diffidence.

"So what do I have the courtesy of seeing you for today?" Rodney asked.

"I need someone to help me with hooking up my video system," Abraham said.

"What kind of system is it?" Rodney asked.

"It's the new centurion3."

"I'm not familiar with that system. It would involve reading the instruction manual, and I'm having a hard time doing that now. Reading is not something I like to do," Rodney said.

"It's a requirement to have a centurion3 in all the tournaments now," Abraham said.

"You've got to be kidding. I just bought my system with the money I saved for a year. Now we're required to buy another one."

"They said online that if you're a dedicated gamer, you won't mind doing it," Abraham replied.

"Well, if they said it online like that, then I guess it's all right."

Rodney handed Abraham a joystick, and they both sat on the couch and began a PVP game. Rodney knew this was going to go well into the night, and he hoped the snacks in the fridge would be enough. Abraham secretly wished Rodney would eventually order out for pizza. They began to talk impulsively about their playing and their game as the night rolled on.

Eventually, Rodney was getting tired as three o'clock came and told Abraham he had had enough for the night. Seeing that there probably would be no pizza, Abraham agreed and finished their current set. They had finished their last bag of potato chips, so Abraham was satisfied to leave. Having a high metabolism, Abraham worried at times about eating Rodney out of house and home. He would eat a ton and still keep his thin build.

When Abraham left, Rodney went into his bedroom and plopped down on the mattress. He hoped he wasn't too wired and could get to sleep so that he could wake up at least before lunch. He lay on the mattress on his stomach, thinking of what his current strategies were for the Jenkins Bros video game. The various equipment and powers of the Jenkins Bros began to roll through his head, and he was unable to sleep for an hour.

* * *

The first thing Rodney did when he woke the next morning was reach for the video game joystick. It gave him comfort to know the joystick was nearby. He looked around for the lost bag of potato chips but gave up after coming to the conclusion that Abraham must have confiscated it. With the joystick in his hand, he contemplated his activities for the day. He knew he had to do a garbage run for the day. He also contemplated the idea of a snack run. He knew he couldn't live off of snacks forever and would need to order meat from a restaurant at some point. His diet was pretty much chips and beef, but he didn't let it bother him.

After a couple of rounds of FantasyDreamFX, Rodney felt he could take on the world. There was something in the pixels and graphics that he felt was telling him things. He was also looking forward to the mail today. He was getting his government check and knew he had to make it to the bank before it closed so that he could cash it. Store hours were becoming more and more hazy to him, but he still kept some kind of semblance of memory about such things.

Later that day, he got on his skateboard and made his way to the bank with his money pouch in hand. Skateboarding was something inherent in him, and he didn't have a problem weaving his way through the streets and traffic. He only wished he knew the closing hours of the bank. He didn't want to make the same trip again.

With the bank in sight at the bottom of the hill, he could tell it was still open by the cars in the parking lot. He decided to play it safe by walking down the hill with his skateboard in hand. He passed an Arabic restaurant that he often went to but decided he would just make his way home that day.

At the bank, he saw that his favorite teller was open, so he went to him to make some idle chatter. The teller's name was Julio, and he gave a smirk when he saw Rodney enter the lobby.

"What can I do for you today, Rodney?" he said in an accent.

"Same-o, same-o," Rodney said and plopped the government check down on the booth.

"Play any new video games?" Julio asked.

"Well, with the new system we're required to have, I'm having to transfer all my old video games into the new format," Rodney said.

"Even Jenkins Bros?" Julio asked.

"Yep."

"Well, I'm sure it's not too long of a process to do all that," Julio countered with a discerning look.

"Just probably a month or two," Rodney surmised.

"Well, here's your cash, Rodney. Don't spend it all in one place," Julio said with a smile and counted out the bills to him.

Rodney stuffed the money into his money pouch and carried his skateboard out of the bank branch. It would be a little climb back up the hill, but there was a lot of interesting downhill avenue on the way home. All he had to worry about was swerving between pedestrians with his skateboard, and he would come across very few on his route home.

When he arrived at his apartment door, he saw a slip of paper stuck to the window. A feeling of alarm rose up in him as he thought it might be an eviction notice. He looked closely and realized it was just a package he needed to sign for.

He realized this could be the new system he was waiting on and put the slip in his pocket. He hoped he would remember where he placed it. His memory wasn't as good as it used to be, although it seemed to be sharp when it came to his video games.

He walked into his apartment and threw his money pouch on the table. He had an immediate impulse to turn on his game system and play a video game, but his hunger pangs in his stomach won out, and he decided to go shopping for food. He didn't use his skateboard when he went grocery shopping. He knew the manager there well and was always able to borrow a shopping cart if he needed it.

He decided to make his way to the post office as well since it wasn't too far away from the grocery store. He knew he would have to borrow a cart this time if he was to get his new video game system. He locked the door to his apartment and began to walk to the grocery store with his money pouch. He didn't have a problem understanding the icons in the traffic signals, but he was less inclined to read the messages on storefronts and bulletins on bulletin boards. He seemed to have to struggle to read these things, so he was beginning to give up on it altogether.

When he reached the post office, he noticed there wasn't the usual line. He always had difficulty with the grouchy old postman at the counter. As soon as he entered the lobby, he reacted with dread when he saw that the old man was there today. He got behind a lady with a package who was offended by the old man's attitude toward her.

He remembered that his postal slip was in his pocket and reached for it. He looked at it with a puzzled expression on his face. He didn't understand the new protocol that the post office was taking toward packages and was reluctant to ask the old clerk any questions.

"Why do I have to pick this up at the post office?" Rodney said.

"If you would read the slip thoroughly, you might understand, but I would guess you young people are having a hard time reading these days!" the old clerk barked at Rodney. "Here, hand it to me."

Rodney handed the slip to the old clerk as he looked at it with disgust.

"The post office has a new policy for video game systems," the old man said. "There have been a series of thefts off of people's porches, and they seem to be only video game systems."

"Well, I don't have a problem coming here to pick them up," Rodney said. "I just wish there was a more convenient way of getting it delivered," Rodney said.

"If you're talking about the new centurion3, you might as well forget about home delivery. Those models have to be signed for, and your packing slip is no exception," the old clerk said.

Rodney didn't like the bossy tone of the old clerk but knew he had to play by the rules, so he cooperated and did what the old man said.

The old man went to the back of the post office's warehouse and came back with the box. Rodney was aglow and began to faun over the box at the counter. The old clerk looked on with disgust at Rodney's tacit admiration of the package. Rodney reached into his money pouch and paid the acceptance charge to the old clerk and placed the video game system into his cart.

He walked out of the post office after deciding not to say thank you to the clerk. He felt he had to make such a statement to reinforce his feelings about his video games and the "video community." He harbored somewhat of anger and resentment against the community of people who looked down on his hobby. He considered them "nerdists."

He made his way to the grocery store and started to think about what type of instant food he was going to get. He couldn't help but eye a gun shop that had opened up near the grocery store. It was called Steve's guns. Ramen noodles were something he always bought, but he usually had meat cravings as well. He didn't always look for discounts and sales, so he usually looked for the cheap brands to buy. Math wasn't his forte, so he made vague estimates about what he was buying.

That night, he managed to hook up his centurion3 with minimal problems. He didn't bother reading the directions as there was a new icon system that explained how to install the system. He began to eat some beef jerky while the whole system downloaded onto his television.

Once the pixels began to show up on the screen, Rodney felt a rush of relief surge through him. The pixels gave him a sense of calm and assurance that he had never known before. He could never read a schematic but decided it probably wasn't necessary with the skills and knowledge he was learning from video games.

He began to look around for the video joystick and began to panic. He couldn't find it. He remembered from an old saying that his father said that "when you can't find something, it usually is in the most obvious place."

His heart began to pound heavily, and he was having a hard time breathing. He desperately began to look under strewn papers and packages but couldn't seem to find it. He checked behind his bed, thinking it may have fallen between the wall and the bed but to no avail. As he began to shout and swear in his growing despair, he looked up at his desk and saw the joystick sitting there.

He couldn't help but feel a little angry at his behavior, but a sense of relief also ruled through him. He was angry at his own inability to keep track of things but was glad the searching was over. He picked up an olive out of a bowl on his coffee table and began to think about what else he needed to be doing. He knew he needed to clean his place up but wasn't quite ready for that yet.

He plopped down on his couch and began his nightly ritual of video games. He couldn't help but feel a little bond with this new system, but he had strong loyalty to the video game company's promotions and directives about the new system. He also had somewhat of loyalty to his video game friends as well.

Besides Abraham, Rodney felt he had an attachment to some of his other video game friends. He had no idea how long he would remain friends with them, but they would come to his pad and play scores of video games with him. Unlike Rodney though, they had other interests and responsibilities in their lives. One of them even played basketball on the high school team. He was expecting a couple of them over Saturday night to test out his new system.

He sat in his chair and stared around the room, trying to get a mental grip on things. He thought of the possibility of his video friends going off to other towns or college or maybe joining the military. He wondered what would happen to him if he was left all alone in town. He couldn't help but think of Steve's guns.

He got up from his chair and grabbed his cell phone to text some of his friends for Saturday night videos. After he finished, he decided to clean up his floor and room. Cleaning up was always a difficult process for Rodney. He would get confused about what to keep and what to throw away.

As he worked on his room, he couldn't help but feel a chill in his bones at his isolation. He stared through the window at the distant wilderness of trees and buildings outside his apartment. He felt he had become a cold person with his ongoing obsession with video games and tried to keep his mind on his cleaning.

He began receiving texts in the late afternoon from his "other" friends. The text messages said things like "I'll be there" or "sounds cool." Rodney was indecisive about which games he would play that night. He knew that one of the players was overly excitable, and he wondered how he would act and react to his selection of video games that night. Rodney decided he would pick exciting video games that the majority would like.

He went to the refrigerator to pour himself a coke into a big drinking bottle he had. All he had for snacks were two bags of potato chips, but he didn't worry too much about the munchies with these guys. Unlike him, they had other interests besides video games. Some liked sports, and one of them was even a former Boy Scout. Rodney took a drink and was not apprehensive at all about his night of video games.

A knock on his back door signaled the first visitor of the night. It was Sonny. He was a former Boy Scout and was wearing his dad's field jacket. He saluted to Rodney and walked into his kitchen.

"You got anything to eat around here?" Sonny said.

"All I have is chips and some coke," Rodney said.

"Well, all I've been eating are MREs. I'm a survivalist, you know. I prepare for the worst," Sonny said.

"Aren't you planning on going to the Army soon? The food would be pretty good there."

"That's three months away."

"Well, I'm keeping my TV dinners for myself," Rodney said.

"Well, I'll take some chips then."

Rodney handed him a bag of potato chips, and Sonny sat down on his couch. Rodney grabbed the joystick and threw it at Sonny and then laid down himself on a beanbag. They both agreed to play Jenkins Brothers on the centurion3.

A knock on Rodney's back door an hour later caused Rodney to get up from his beanbag and answer the door. It was his friend Wallis from the basketball court. Rodney had befriended him after watching him play and talking to him on the sidelines. Wallis had gained an interest in Rodney's video game obsession. Rodney's description of some of the video games interested Wallis. Rodney would then invite Wallis to his pad.

Wallis walked in and nodded his head at Rodney.

"Hey, bro, I told you I'd be here in a minute."

Wallis looked at Sonny and immediately felt a little uncomfortable with him there. Sonny's beard and field jacket were the signs of his fear, but he brushed it off and held out his hand in greeting. Sonny shook his head but didn't say anything.

They sat down, and Rodney began to coach them about the centurion3 and the Jenkins Bros video game, and all of them began to settle down for a good night of gaming. As they played, they began to crack jokes and make comments about the game and began to feel comfortable around each other.

After an hour or so, a knock came on their door again, and Rodney got up to answer it. It was Charlie. This is the one that Rodney thought might be affected by the violent videos.

"Good time, Charlie!" Rodney said.

Charlie walked in with a beaming smile on his face. He was the type that tried his hardest to please what he thought were the "cool" ones. He would go out of his way to be subservient to Rodney up to the point of Rodney's annoyance.

"What are the games tonight?" Charlie said with a smile plastered on his face.

"We're using the centurion3 for Jenkins Bros brawl. If you're interested, you'll have to wait for your turn with the joystick. I only have three," Rodney said.

"Hey, Sonny," Charlie said.

Sonny responded with a look of feigned tolerance on his face. Charlie looked confused at Sonny's response. He began to become focused on the video game that was being played by Sonny and Wallis. He began to shake his hands in a nervous joy at the video game. He did this when he was excited about something, and the other guys seemed to notice this nervousness.

As Sonny, Wallis and Rodney continued to be involved in their game, Charlie continued to wring his hands in excitement. Sonny and Wallis had figured out some of the basic tactics that the game had to offer. Charlie understood the prompts and tactics and began to shout exclamations and advice to the other guys, "You shouldn't have done that, Sonny. Oh, Wallis, that was your big chance!"

As the game got more intense, Charlie became more excited and started to wail at the intense images on the TV monitor.

"Woo-hoo! Woo-hoo!" he exclaimed, and the others started to become alarmed at his rantings. In a short while, Charlie got up from his beanbag and began to jump around the room as he continued to wail.

Rodney, Sonny, and Wallis all looked at each other, somewhat confused at the situation. Rodney decided to take the lead and follow Charlie as he began to wail and hop into the kitchen. Rodney walked past Charlie and opened the kitchen's back door, and Charlie wailed and hopped through it.

"These games are awesome! I've got such a rush!"

Rodney closed the door and locked it and walked back into the room where the other video gamers congregated.

"I don't know if that's the last we'll see of him, but maybe we can get this campaign arc done before the grills close," Rodney said.

When the final video melee was resolved, they all began to talk to each other about their lives.

"I'm planning on joining the military this fall, so I guess I'll be out of the video thing for a while," Sonny said.

"My family is moving to another state, so I guess I won't be in the coven either," Wallis said.

Rodney was silent for a minute, thinking about this change of events. He was a little angry but tried not to show it. He thought about Abraham and hoped he still had him as a video friend. He rubbed his nose and decided to reply.

"I don't have too many friends interested in videos. I hope I can find some more."

Sonny and Wallis laughed and began to joke.

"I guess this is a major disruption in your life. Have you thought about getting another hobby?" Sonny said.

At times, Sonny and Wallis would tease Rodney about things. He took the jabs because he wanted to keep them as video friends. Now he didn't have a reason to hang around them anymore, so he delivered his ultimatum.

"I think it's time to break up our video group. I'll keep in touch with you on Facebook, but I don't think I'll have much to say to you there if you're no longer interested in video games."

Wallis and Sonny looked at each other but didn't say anything and got up from their beanbags and walked toward the kitchen. As they walked out, Rodney began to think about his situation. Loneliness and isolation were the feelings that began to emerge in him. He began to watch the television and the provocative images that it invoked. He felt a resentment to the outside world that he couldn't shake from his mind.

He began to nervously eat the remaining potato chips on his plate, thinking about the current change of events and how it was affecting him. Feelings of anger, resentment, frustration, and alienation began to consume him. He looked around at the dimly lit room and the dreariness. He looked at his skateboard and saw the bright colors that beckoned and urged him to revitalize his youthful energy. He took the skateboard to the kitchen back door and threw it down on the steps and began to ride his way to Steve's gun shop.

A Conspiracy of Charlatans

The night wore on as Jesse, Will, Fred, Amy, and Susan worked on their contraption in the woods near the Wilson farm. The Wilson farm at one time was a bustling farm with a full family operating it. Charlie Wilson was the firstborn in the family who was the only one left that ran the farm. Once he had two siblings, a brother and a sister, and both parents to help run the farm. They grew corn, tobacco, and okra and had a dairy business with chickens and cows. His parents eventually passed away, and his brother died in the last war with only his sister left, who got a job in the civil service and moved away.

The five charlatans knew about Charlie's farm for some time now because of his occasional visits to his town's church. All were members of his church and considered Charlie a little on the strange and reclusive side. They were all budding members of the science club at school and decided to make their special contraption as a prank on Charlie. It was a certain "conspiracy" of theirs that they wanted to bring to some conclusion.

"What kind of contraption is this anyway? All you had me do is gather the materials for it," Jesse said.

"It's used to project an image in the sky," Amy said.

All the members of the youth gang were a bedraggled lot. They had an unkempt look with only jeans, T-shirts, and tennis shoes as their clothing. Amy's T-shirt had a picture of a cocker spaniel on it, while Jesse's T-shirt showed an unhappy face with a bleeding bullet hole.

"Do you think that farm man will be fooled by this projector?"

"I hope so. We worked long and hard in my garage perfecting the holographic image projector," Fred said.

The contraption was on a toy wagon that the gang copped from Will's younger brother. They were careful not to roll it too hard to make a loud sound. It was past midnight now, and they wanted their hard-won plot to work its dark tendrils on Charlie's farm.

They noticed a light in the window of the living room of the farm. They assumed that was where Charlie was residing.

The holographic image projector began to spurt strange sounds as its electrodes heated up for the oncoming show for Charlie. Fred had spent some time creating images he thought might "spook" Charlie and tested such illusions at his own house in his backyard. He had the help of Amy and Will, with Will doing a lot of the design work. Amy was basically the scientific consultant and helped Fred with the illusory images.

The moon was not out that night, so the charlatans had to rely on starlight to conduct their secret conspiracy. They whispered among each other as they positioned the contraption near the woods of Charlie's farm.

"Do you think he is in his living room tonight?" Jesse asked Susan.

"I know a little bit about his doings from his uncle at church," Susan said. "He likes to relax in his living room on Saturday nights staring out the window at times."

Susan was sort of the spy of the group, and they needed her for her "social skills." She could find out about people by befriending them and gaining information about Charlie from the people at the church. The main source of information was Charlie's uncle, who also went to the church.

"I think I got everything I could glean from Charlie's uncle about his personal schedule and goings-on at his house. I've learned that he goes into town to trade once a week but spends a lot of time by himself in his main room overlooking his farm at night," Susan said.

"That's why we're here tonight, isn't it?" Jesse asked.

"We're here tonight for our conspiracy," Amy answered.

"Do you think we'll be able to project that holographic image tonight?" Will asked.

"I'm sure of it," Amy replied. "All we have to do is project the image in the sky above his lawn to show the flying creature we're trying to fool him with."

"I made the flying creature with tentacles and oversized wings. Do you think these things will show up clearly outside?" Fred said.

"They should be able to if all goes well," Amy answered.

They began to drag the contraption through the woods behind Charlie's farm, and using a navigator's tool, they positioned it in the way they wanted and waited for Jesse to sneak down to the house and give a signal.

Light crept from Charlie's living room window as Jesse waited for some kind of stirring inside the farmhouse. He saw the light go off in the upstairs bedroom window and, according to Susan's account of his schedule, would make his way down to the living room. Jesse signaled to the others at the contraption to convene their illusory designs.

The contraption began to project the monster near the treetops and to move its dark form in various silhouettes across the dark forest. Jesse watched for Charlie's reaction near the window and noticed he did get his attention when he made various noises in the yard. That was the plan, and Jesse eventually saw Charlie peer out the window in amazement at what he saw high above the treetops.

Jesse contacted the others on his cell phone. "I think our plan is working. He's looking outside at our flying polyp."

Quiet, sustained fits of laughter were heard among the other four members of the conspiracy as their "flying polyp" did its dance. "Flying polyp" was the name they decided to call it because of Will's knowledge of monsters.

Jesse leaned on the fence and thought about what was happening at Charlie's farm. He watched as Charlie walked outside and gazed at the "polyp" with an amazed but also amused look. He knew then that they had not completely convinced Charlie of any strange doings at his farm. He watched him walk back into the house with a chuckle as Jesse lowered his head in disappointment and began to walk back to the others with the disheartening news.

When he reached the others, Amy was the first to appear in the darkness and question his scouting skills, "How did he take it?"

Jesse looked at her with a stern expression.

"I don't think he believes it," Jesse answered.

"We probably are going to need to devise another plan of Lovecraftian proportions to convince him of something akin to the supernatural."

Jesse was used to Amy speaking in this arcane way and didn't let it bother him. He knew she was somewhat of the leader of the group, and he reluctantly answered to her occasional dictations.

"Does Will have any ideas?" Jesse countered.

"I'll ask him," Amy walked back to the others and explained to them what Jesse said.

The others listened to Amy's question and waited for a response from Will. Will sat in front of the campfire they had built for themselves and pensively thought about it. Will was the tall one of the group and the king of practical jokes among his friends. Susan and Fred tended to take orders from Will and Amy but also had ideas of their own as well.

"I think if we created some kind of construct of the polyp like an egg or some kind of carapace that it shed and placed it in his fields, he might sit up and take notice," Fred said.

"I think if we found a way to make scratching noises on his roof, that could sway his opinion about other worldly things," Will offered.

Amy agreed and decided to take the helm of the brainstorming session.

"I think we need to immediately get to work on these constructs and devise a plan about creating otherworldly sounds at night to convince Charlie of an otherworldly presence at his home."

They all began to stamp out the hidden campfire in the woods near Charlie's farm and carried their contraption back to Will's truck.

* * *

Charlie walked back into the house, thinking about the nightmarish "vision" he beheld outside in the night sky. He assumed it was some prank that maybe a neighbor created, but he was not sure. He was not easily spooked by such things and decided to turn his mind to more pressing concerns.

The taxman held a lien on his house because of unpaid taxes. He was trying to make a go of his farming but knew in this day and age, farming was becoming a lost art. He had to give his deed up to the courthouse as part of the deal with the county judge and that he would pay his taxes before he would get his deed back. He was thinking of changing to tobacco instead of the edible vegetables that he had to grow—anything to bring a profit.

He sat down at his desk and did his accounting work for the farm. He knew if he kept a good tally of his expenses and income and some kind of numbers in his mind, he would have a better chance at holding his farm.

He finished some farm figures at his desk, still thinking about the strange occurrence at his farm. He tried to make sense of it all and decided he would talk to the pastor about the matter this Sunday. He was on good terms with the pastor and always found him helpful and considerate.

He thought about calling his sister tonight just to have a friendly word with her. He was on good terms with her, and maybe she could help explain the strange occurrences at his farm. She always remained a little aloof from the family and only seemed to be involved in her own affairs, but she would always listen to him offer a little advice.

When he was finished with his phone call with his sister, he retired to his bed for the night. She seemed a little spooked about what he told her, and he almost regretted talking to her about it. What he ended up doing was reassuring her that it probably was just a figment in his mind. She had always complained before about his "figmenting" and overactive imagination. She thought he imagined things happening when they didn't and jumping to conclusions. Charlie didn't really feel he was that way but tried not to argue with her. He beat his pillow and tried his best to get some sleep.

* * *

Will, Amy, and Susan sat in Will's living room, thinking of the constructs and sound effects they would make. Will came from a family that had plenty of capital and resources to be able to pull pranks on people. Amy seemed to be the one with the least conscience about the whole conspiracy.

"I think we could make some kind of eggs to scatter around his farm and what could look like shed skin or a carapace of the polyp that Fred could help paint and sculpt. I know my dad's career in plastics would allow us to make those constructs," Will said.

"What about drones to land on his roof?" Amy said.

"To make the sound effects?"

"We could think of some kind of regimented program that all the drones would follow to duplicate clawing sounds on his roof as if the flying polyp landed there."

"It would have to be at night," Will said. "That way, he wouldn't necessarily be able to tell they were drones."

"Maybe we could do it after he's gone to bed and have them fly away before he has a chance to get outside," Susan interjected.

"Well, whatever it is, we need to get working on the constructs now to keep everything within a reasonable time frame," Amy commanded.

"I'll tell Fred to start on some kind of molds for the carapaces and eggs, and I'll get to work on making some of my drones into noisemakers. If we work together as a team, we can get this done in a little while," Will said.

Amy and Susan walked out of the living room, talking and joking among themselves and planning the month's schedule for the group. Will contacted Fred on his cell phone, and Fred answered quickly.

"What do you think about this conspiracy of ours?" Will asked Fred.

"I think it's all right if it doesn't get too far out of hand."

"In what way?"

"Too sinister. Y' know?"

"Well, I'm okay with it if it gets a few laughs," Will replied.

"I just hope we're joking around about the right things," Fred said.

"I don't think it's too bad. Do you think you could have those molds made by the end of the week?"

"I think so."

"Well, I'm going to call Jesse now, so I'll see you."

Will hung up and called Jesse.

"Hey, Will," Jesse answered.

"Have you talked to Susan about Charlie's schedule and when you can do your scouting?" Will said.

"I don't know why I have to be the one who does the scouting all the time. I would like to learn how to make some of the devices you all make. I feel my job is a bit below my station," Jesse said.

"You can help Fred with the molds if you want."

"What exactly are we trying to accomplish here anyway?" Jesse asked.

"You'll have to talk to Amy about that," Will answered.

"Well, I'll talk to Susan about Charlie's activities and try to get some scouting done this week. I think I could find out why he goes to the shed all the time with my new binoculars," Jesse said.

"We'll see you," Will said and hung up.

Will sat in his living room, pondering the group's conspiracy and then brushed off any pensive thoughts he might have and decided to do a little work in the workshop.

* * *

Charlie woke from his slumber and gave himself his normal breakfast meal: a little cereal, coffee, and toast. He hoped he would not have to resort to a diet of pork and beans in the near future, and the business with the taxes and the bank would be resolved soon but knew not to count his eggs before they're hatched.

He decided to head to the shed to get rid of the nagging feeling he had every so often about his hobby. He would worry about where some of the painting tools he had were stored and was usually heading to the shed to find them when he couldn't find them anywhere else. Painting with oil paints was the only consuming hobby he had in his spare time, and time was becoming hard to come by.

He walked out to the shed and unlocked the shed lock with his key and opened the creaky door. Using his flashlight, he began to sift through the cardboard boxes of paints and brushes until he was satisfied with their placement and location. He looked to the back of the shed at the few easels he had and what he had painted. He would do his painting behind a grove of apple trees in the afternoon, and it was then that he decided to carry them out of the shack to the grove.

In the distance, Jesse watched with his binoculars and began to get an idea of Charlie's hobbies. He wondered what he would tell the others and what they would think about this new revelation. He closed up his binoculars and decided to end his scouting for the day.

* * *

Amy and Susan began to debate when to lay down the carapaces and eggs. They knew it had to be done at a time when the drones would begin to drum the roof. This would connect the two incidents together and maybe convince Charlie of strange doings at his farm.

They decided, with the exception of Will, they would do the transplanting of the polyp's constructs after Charlie retired for the night. When they were finished, Jesse would give the signal to Will, and Will would start his drones to make their roof-racket. Hopefully, this would wake Charlie, and he would soon discover the eggs and carapaces on his farm.

Amy called Fred on the phone and asked him about the molds, "I've nearly got everything finished and will do a little printing tomorrow."

"Well, don't think that you have to be a Picasso. We need to get this done by the end of the week," Amy said.

"I don't think we'll have too much of a problem scattering these things across his property. I just hope we can do it without being seen."

"It will be when he's sleeping if Susan is right about this."

"I just hope Susan will be able to help you and Jesse with putting the constructs on his farm. I'll be with Will and the drones."

"I'll make sure Susan is pulling her own weight out there," Amy replied.

* * *

That night, they all gathered at Will's house and went over their plan. Jesse would have to act as the scout as well as the distributor of the constructs. He had Amy and Susan to help him but was a little worried about how stealthy and quiet they would be with the placing of the constructs.

Will was discussing with Fred how they would control the drones with remotes after they received a Morse code signal from Jesse's flashlight. They didn't think their plan was very difficult with their knowledge of electronics, but they still were a little apprehensive.

They all piled into a van with their "conspiracy materials" and made out for Charlie's farm. They were all eating sandwiches that Susan made except for the driver, Amy. As she was driving, she was explaining in her usual bossy way all of what was going to "go down" that night.

"Now let's remember our individual duties and the timeline for tonight. Things should run smoothly if we all do what we're supposed to do," Amy said.

"Well, I don't want to be the only one throwing all the carapaces and eggs on his fields. You all need to be doing it too, so I will be able to do my scouting," Jesse said.

"I'm glad this stuff is not too heavy. I'm not as cut out for this work as the rest of you," Susan said.

"It shouldn't be too hard. Just remember we've got to remain quiet. Keep it stealthy," Jesse said.

Once the van reached the farm, it was late into the night. All members of the conspiracy helped with unloading the eggs and carapaces on the road next to Charlie's farm. Will and Fred got into the front seat after Susan, Jesse, and Amy departed from the van with Will in the driver's seat, yelling through the window, "We'll pick you up here in about three hours." They drove off to their designated launching point for their drones.

Amy, Susan, and Jesse talked among each other in hushed tones about how they would distribute the constructs. They decided they would put the majority of it in his fields and maybe some of it in the hills and near the lake where he went fishing. Jesse took a bagful and headed near Charlie's farmhouse. He knew he had to rely on Amy's rudimentary Morse code signals to determine when she and Susan were finished.

They worked for two hours when Amy sent her signal to Jesse. Relieved that they were finished, Jesse sent his signal to Will and Fred to begin their drone attack on the roof of Charlie's farm. All was running smoothly when Will and Fred finally launched their drones. Jesse made a dash back to the van rendezvous point, where hopefully, he would meet Susan and Amy.

The drones began to make their scraping sounds on the roof when Fred and Will saw the light come on in the upstairs bedroom window of Charlie's farmhouse. Will and Fred decided to do their drone dance on Charlie's roof for just a short while, and then they would get in their van and head to the rendezvous point.

When they got their drones back into the van, they saw in the distance a lone figure come out the back door of the farmhouse. It was Charlie. Holding a rifle in his hand, he shouted toward the van, "You kids, stop your tomfoolery and pranks and get off my property!"

Fred and Will piled into the van and raced off to the rendezvous point.

"Do you think we blew our cover?" Fred said.

"Once he sees the eggs and carapaces, he will probably think differently. We worked hard on making them realistic."

"This whole thing is stupid. I don't think we've fooled him at all," Fred replied.

"We'll find out probably how well our prank went when Susan goes to church and talks with the preacher. I've heard Charlie confides in him on occasion," Will said.

The van pulled up to the rendezvous point where Amy and Susan were waiting. Fred and Will opened their doors and greeted them with curt nods. Susan and Amy were slightly nervous about the situation.

"We haven't seen Jesse," Amy said.

"He should be here in a little while," Will replied.

"I don't think he has that far to travel," Fred said.

They waited by the road for a short period of time before Jesse appeared. He held his hands up to assure everyone that everything was all right.

He then began to explain what he saw, "I don't know what you all have seen, but Charlie was clearly upset. I heard him yelling with a gun in his backyard fields. I'm not sure if he is such a believer in our conspiracy."

"I'll be able to tell when I talk with the preacher. My parents are good friends with him, and I can find out about things like that," Susan said with a smug tone.

They all drove home in the van, disheartened by their plot to fool Charlie. Amy seemed to be the only one who was still enthusiastic about the whole affair. They all decided that what they could learn from Susan would help in determining if their hoax was successful.

Amy then began to lecture to the group, "If we could pull off a hoax like that successfully, who knows what we could do next. All the richest, most successful people in the world were professional hucksters. They knew how to pull off a successful hoax. Once we've done something like that, we will be on the way to a better life. Agreed?"

The others responded with reluctant nods, with the exception of Jesse. Jesse pondered the whole situation and replied, "I would like to go with Susan to find out what she can from the preacher."

"I don't think that will be a good idea," Amy said.

"I can do these things very well on my own," Susan said.

SURVEYS AND SCAMS

"Oh, I'll just wait out in the car. I won't interfere with your discussion," Jesse said.

"Okay, Jesse." Susan smiled. "But let me do my work."

With that, the group disbanded after they reached Will's house. Will and Fred still had work to do with the drones, but the rest had to think of excuses for their parents. Jesse never had to worry about that with the single mom he went home to.

* * *

"Well, it's already been settled," the preacher told Susan. "The bank is working with the local courts to confiscate his deed and property. Charlie can't come up with the thousand dollars needed to keep his property."

Susan tried to keep a facade of ignorance in front of the preacher as she divulged her information from him.

"Doesn't he have a sister that could help him?"

"She seems to think the farm is haunted or being invaded by some creature. She saw what she thought were eggs and what looked like shed skins or shells on the property. She wants Charlie to move out. Charlie has tried to convince her that it's just a prank by some kids, but she doesn't believe it yet," the preacher explained.

"Well, maybe if it is haunted, he does need to move out. What do you think is going on at his farm?" Susan asked the preacher.

"I would hate to think there are kids playing a prank on Charlie, but that may be the case," the preacher said.

"Well, I hope the best for Charlie, but I have to go home now. I have chores to do," Susan said and stood up from the community table and walked to the church door.

"We'll see you at the next church service, Susan," the preacher said as Susan nodded and walked out the door.

Waiting at the car was Jesse, who was full of questions for Susan.

"What does the preacher know about Charlie?" he asked.

"Charlie has a lot of money problems and is probably going to lose the farm. The incident we created was pretty much the last straw."

Jesse sat against the car and thought about the situation. "Well, we've been busy making things tough for Charlie with our conspiracy. What if we came up with a good conspiracy?"

"A good conspiracy?"

"Yeah, a conspiracy that was good instead of bad."

"A good conspiracy! Yeah!" Susan's eyes brightened with an agreement.

"What do you think the conspiracy could involve?"

"Maybe we could conspire to have his debts paid and get his deed back from the bank," Susan said.

"In order to be a conspiracy, it would still have to be secretive."

"We'll discuss this with Amy, Fred, and Will at our next meeting to figure out how we're going to do this," Jesse said as they both got into their car.

* * *

Amy called the minutes to the meeting and made roll call. All were present, and Jesse decided to lead the discussion.

"Susan and I have thought of the idea of a good conspiracy. Where the conspirators would do a good deed to the one they're plotting against."

"What's this all about? I've never heard of anything like that. You can't get what you want by plotting good deeds," Amy said.

"Well, we're not in agreement with everything you say. We think a good conspiracy against Charlie would help all involved in numerous ways. We could help pay his debts at the bank and get his deed back from the courthouse," Jesse said.

"How would this help all involved?" Amy said.

"How would we help anyone by doing a bad conspiracy?" Jesse replied.

"Well, we'll vote on it and see what everyone thinks," Amy suggested with a taunting tone. "Who agrees that we should have the bad conspiracy raise their hands?"

Will and Fred looked at each other and decided not to raise their hands. Amy was immediately shocked when she was the only one to raise her hand.

"All those in favor of a good conspiracy raise your hand."

All but Amy raised their hands.

"The good conspiracy has it. Let's get to work."

* * *

Will and Fred were put in charge of disseminating flyers throughout the town that would ask for donations for Charlie's farm. They decided to use their drones to drop flyers all around town while Susan and Jesse would work with the bank and eventually the courthouse to get Charlie's deed back.

Amy was put to work as a scout.

The first week, no money was sent to the PO box they set up. Then in the second week, checks started to come in slowly, and by the third week, they had the money. It would only be a matter of days before the debt collectors would make their visit, so Jesse and Susan knew they had to act fast.

They visited the bank to cash the checks and then went to the courthouse to get the farm's deed after showing that the debt was paid. They were asked a few questions by the clerk, but everything turned out more smoothly than they thought.

All five of the conspirators showed up at the preacher's door the day before Charlie would have to face the judge. They began to explain their good conspiracy to the preacher and their decision to restore Charlie's farm. The preacher was pleased with what he heard and gave them a holy smile.

"I think Charlie will consider this good conspiracy as an act of angels and herald the occasion as providence. I will give him the deed tonight and keep your conspiracy a secret as all good conspiracies should be."

He led them out of the church, but they all decided to keep Amy as a scout at Charlie's farm to make sure that the preacher did deliver the deed. Amy had insisted on this. As the day broke, they knew their conspiracy was successful, and they ended up celebrating at the local steak house with the excess money.

"Do you think good conspiracies really do any good?" Will asked Jesse that night.

"They might actually change the course of history. Who knows?" Jesse answered.

Amy was eating her steak by herself at a separate table.

"Will we try this again, or should we disband?" Will asked.

"I think we should disband before we all get too greedy and want something more than a good conspiracy," Fred said.

Will then stood up at the table and made a proclamation.

"In this year of our Lord, I ask that all who wish to disband the group raise their hands and say 'Aye.'" All but Amy raised their hands in favor of disbanding the group.

"The votes have it. We are officially disbanded," Will said.

They all walked out of the steakhouse with Amy in tow. Jesse whispered to Susan, "Keep an eye on Amy. I don't think she's completely come around yet." Susan agreed, and they all piled into the van to say their last goodbyes to each other for a good deed done.

The Hard-liners

The obese woman clerk looked with a discerning frown on her face as the four old men walked into the hamburger and biscuit restaurant. They all talked with a southern drawl and wore blue jeans with leather cowboy boots and sneakers and thick leather belts with their names inscribed on them. They usually came to this restaurant in the morning for the biscuits and to talk about things they were most knowledgeable about: hunting, fishing, and maybe their company jobs or contracting work. They all sat down at a table and began talking about some of their various maladies and the weather.

"This heat is getting rough for me. My air-conditionin' broke down last week, an' I haven't gawt it fixed hyet," the tall one with the beard named TJ said.

"With the way my jawb is, ma back is lucky to be workin' at awl. Ah've had to have three operations in the last three years," the shorter one with a shrill voice named Jake said. He paused and added to TJ, "How wus that colonoscopy you had last week?"

"Ah was shittin' all afternoon before the test," TJ said.

"That ain't nothin' to write home about. If you gawt a wife goin' through chemotherapy, yer pretty much dun' in," said Jake. "We jus' awta be glad we have the cump'ny health insurance we have, or we would be up the creek," Jake said.

They all were silent for a while as they ate their breakfast of biscuits and gravy. They always hung out at this restaurant because of the biscuits. In their opinion, these were the best biscuits in town. The women that cooked them would put their heart and soul into making these biscuits, and some would receive commendations from the restaurant or maybe the local newspaper for their hard work.

"Didn't the doctor tell you to lay off biscuits and gravy?" Randy, the younger one, chided TJ.

"Well, what am I supposed to eat if I can't eat biscuits and gravy?"

"I think we need to change the subject," Randy said. He was always the diplomatic one that knew how to lead the others into better conversations.

"Well, ah, thank my job is getting the best of me." Percy was usually the silent one but decided to speak up.

"Didn't you tell me you gawt a higher pay raise so naw you been able to leave tips at fancy restaurants?" Randy encouraged Percy.

"Yeah, but every waitress ah leave a tip to looks confused about it. L'ak, they don't even know what to dew with it," Percy said.

"Maybe you don't leave a big enuff tip," Randy said, and the others laughed.

"Ah think Percy is a good tipper," Jake said to de-escalate the situation after he had his laugh.

"What do you think about these scammers out here tryin' to scam young people out of their money with their literature and fancy gadgets and toys?" Randy said.

"Well, ah've still got a lot of my toys from way, way back," TJ said. "Don't you think it makes life more livable to have thangs lak that?"

"These kids spend their money on stuff lak that when they could spend it more constructively on somethin' lak a bike or huntin' rifle," Randy stressed.

"Well, ah liked comic books when I wus' growin' up and didn't see anythin' wrong with it," Jake said.

"I'm not talkin' about that. Ah'm talkin' about kids that read those intellectual books and steer them in the wrong direction with its politics," Randy said.

"Ah thank your raht about that," Percy interjected. "They start to baleevin' they're not to blame for their own mistakes. That it's the system or somethin' that's to blame."

The other three nodded their heads in agreement over Percy's remark. The clerk behind the counter gave a disproving look at the old man but continued to take orders from the small line of customers filing in. The old men continued to eat their biscuits and sausage gravy, waiting for Randy to make a quip and lead them into another conversation.

"Ah betcha a kid lak that couldn't last three days in ma factory," Jake said.

"Ah think we could awl agree to that," Randy said. "But that leads me to somethin' else ah want to talk about." He paused for a second and then began, "We need to gather for discussions that illuminate and enlighten our minds more. These times call for more intelligent and honest debates with meaningful and substantive outcomes."

"Ah thank talkin' about my health is jus' as important as any kand of politickin'," TJ said.

"Yeah, but it's politickin' that leads to better types of health plans fer awl of us," Jake said in his shrill, high voice.

"If yew think politickin' is gonna git me any better health plans than wut I gawt, your sadly mistakin'," TJ angrily replied.

"We don't have to talk about health plans, you know," Randy said.

"Well, no matter what we talk about, Ah'm always left out of the conversation," Percy said.

"You're just the strong and silent type," Jake quipped.

"It could be he's just too dumb to know what to say," Randy said.

They all laughed except Percy, who took the jab in silence. He ate his biscuits and brooded while the others continued to talk.

"You know ah think Percy might be the smartest one of awl of us," TJ said to try to keep Percy out of his doldrums. "Percy is always the odd man out because he is an independent thinker."

"Ah think the way I want to think and don't feel I have anything to lecture others about," Percy said.

This caught Randy off guard and made him think twice about trying to chide Percy about anything in the future. The others always felt like Randy was the leader of this talking group of hard-liners that met in the biscuit and breakfast restaurant in a small southern town. Randy was the most prosperous one of the group with a good-paying job in a hydraulics plant in the next county. Percy worked as a craftsman in the small-town furniture plant.

"Well, if we can't talk politics, wut about religion," Randy decided to change the conversation.

"We're all Baptists except for Percy, who's a Presbyterian."

"Ah guess that leaves him out of the conversation," Jake joked to the others.

"What is it about Presbyterians that are different from Baptists anyway?" TJ asked.

"Ah think they b'leive in baptizin' someone before they even know what's happenin' to 'im," Randy said.

"Ya mean raht after they've been born?" Jake asked.

"Ah think so. Is that true, Percy?" Randy taunted Percy.

"Come by and listen to a sermon an' find out," Percy said.

"Are women supposed to submit to men lak the Bible teaches. 'Cus ah wudn't dare go if that warn't true," TJ said.

"Well, I decided to become a Presbyterian myself because ah like they're preachin'," Percy replied.

"Ah think he chose them because they're more high falootin' than Baptists, an' Percy wuz lookin' for something like that," Jake said.

"You would think I would be the one who would go to a church like that because of my pay scale," Randy said.

"Well, I think we should lay off Percy. If he likes the Presbyterians, that's his business," TJ said in a rare moment of compassion among the hard-liners.

"Well, for one thing, last sermon, they talked about this rich person who made books to teach people how to think lak a rich person. He explained that you would be better off if you were a contrarian and disagreed with people. That's what a rich person does," Percy said. "And then the preacher went on to say that that guy was tellin' people wrong."

"Ah know I don't like it when someone is so contrary to anything I might say. That's not loving your neighbor as yourself. Ah also don't like people who git' this suspicious attitude when you act friendly to them. They think you're after their money or somethin'," Percy continued.

"Well, I'm suspicious of people who act friendly to me. Ah guess it's because of my high-pay scale," Randy said.

"Maybe you'd like those rich man's books," TJ interjected. Jake and Percy laughed.

"Well, I've got to head awn out. Ah've got my work to do," Randy said.

"You're not mad at us, are ya?" TJ said.

"No, not really. It's more about my watch. I've got to git to my job."

"Well, we wouldn't want to interfere with that," Percy said.

* * *

The next morning, all were there except Randy, and they sat at their usual table, which was different from the booths. They had their usual biscuits and sausage and gravy and coffee as the cashier delivered the meals to them. Percy was the first to strike up a conversation this time.

"With Randy gone, d'you thank we could vote on a couple of thangs now?"

"What do yew mean? We're not a club or anything," Jake replied.

"Ah jus' hav' some things ah want to get clear with all of us," Percy said.

"Ah don't want to cause any problems with Randy now," TJ said cautiously.

"Well, Randy seems to want to run everything when he's here, and I thought we could talk about some talkin' points that need to be talked about."

"Well, go ahead, but I don't think Randy is going to like it," Jake said.

"Well, one talkin' point I'd like to discuss is the lack of leadership this group has. Ah don't like it when Randy brags about his high-paying job and the fact that he makes it as easy as he can on himself. It sounds to me that he does a lot of loafin' around on the job and gets paid good for it. That's not setting a good example for the rest of us. A leader should show all his good qualities," Percy said.

"It sounds to me lak you's is wantin' to be the leader," TJ said.

Percy ignored this and continued talking, "He also brags a lot about his affairs with women. That doesn't sound like good qualities to me. Another talkin' point ah'd lak to discuss are the conversations he leads us into. He leads us into politics and politickin' quite a bit. If you want my personal opinion, ah-m sick of politics. Ah personally know a lot about plants and various fauna but never get a chance to discuss it with you all."

"Well, how often does bot'ny come up in conversation, my friend?" Jake replied.

"Are you a little jealous of Randy?" TJ asked.

"Ah just don't understand the conversations that we're led into. That's all." Percy said.

"Well, ah think Randy is a man of great ambitions and success and deserves awl the money he gets," Jake said in his shrill voice.

"He's too much of a hotshot," Percy said.

"That's wut we need in this world. Hotshots," TJ said.

"Ah've made it this far without having to be a hotshot. Ah werk very hard as a cabinetmaker and don't take no shit from no one. The last thing ah want to do is play the field around town with women I don't know. You spread syphilis and AIDS that way. Personally, ah thank the people that get syphilis deserve it with their immoral ways."

"That's jus' the way hotshots are. They look to play the field and fuel their ego. Everyone has an ego to satisfy, y' know? Even you, Percy," TJ said.

"Ah don't need to do thangs lak that to make myself feel better," Percy replied.

SURVEYS AND SCAMS

"You don't get feelings lak that every so often?" TJ asked.

"Now you're getting personal," Percy answered.

"Well, with Randy not here to speak for himself, ah don't think it's right to talk about him like this. You know what the Bible says about judging," Jake said.

"Well, Randy does a whole lot of judgin' himself. We have a right to judge if he's a-doin' it first," Percy replied.

"Lak I said, Randy is not here to defend himself, so it's best we didn't talk about him."

They all sat for a while and ate their biscuits, waiting for someone to lead them into another conversation. They seemed to be without direction, without someone to be a catalyst for conversation. They knew they were missing Randy as their group leader.

Percy opened his mouth once to try to say something but closed it after a while, forgetting what he was going to say. Jake and TJ ate their biscuits in silence. After a while, a woman from behind the counter that usually served them their biscuits came over and offered them some coffee. They were all eager to hear from someone else and accepted her offer of coffee.

"You boys seem to be out of things to say today?" the woman said.

"We were looking for someone lak you to come along," TJ said.

"Well, I'm only here to serve you food, remember that," the waitress said.

They all laughed, and Percy asked the waitress, "Do you have any idea of anything we could talk about?"

"Well, let me think now." The waitress held her pencil up to her mouth and pondered.

"Have you all been watching the news lately? Maybe you could discuss politics. It's the year of election, you know."

"Politickin' is something we're tryin' to get out of talkin' about," Percy said.

"Well, we live in a town where there is not a lot of political action goin' on. You don't see a lot of protests or strikin' goin' on. Maybe you could all start some kind of political action committee."

"Now don't try to be funny, Kay. We're serious about our mornin' discussions," Jake said.

"Well, I'm stumped. Yuns'es just gonna have to figure it out for yourself."

She put her order book back into her apron and picked up the coffee pot and headed back to the kitchen.

Jake, TJ, and Percy sat in silence, thinking about what to think about. They were quiet, drinking their coffee and scraping up the last vestiges of their biscuits and gravy.

"Well, there's no use to wrack our brains about it. We'll jus' wait till Randy comes back," TJ said.

* * *

Several mornings later, all four of them were at a table again, talking about the coming hunting expedition they were going to have. The idea was Percy's, and they all talked about the gear they would take with them on this excursion. All of them had the regular cam-outfits that go with their hunting gear. Percy was the only one that didn't like wearing a hunting hat. Randy, as usual, was bragging about his collection of guns and his ability to hunt with a bow and arrow. The rest had to deal with the hunting rifles they owned and the fact that they didn't have telescopic sights like Randy.

"You know jus' because you got telescopic sights doesn't mean you're the better hunter. Awl it means is you got an easier time catchin' game. The rest of us have to hunt with regular rifles. This means were more perfishint,'" Percy said.

"Ah'm awl about convenience and makin' things as easy as I can for myself," Randy replied.

"Ah'd lak to try that telescopic sight sometime jus' to see how better a hunter I could be," TJ surmised.

"Ah'd rather hunt lak they did in the old days. With jus' a basic hunting rifle," Percy said.

"Ah do that too with my bow and arrow. Ah hunt the way the ancients did. You can't get much older than that," Randy said.

"Yeah, but they didn't have a fancy-schmancy arrow set that yew got. They probably made it themselves," Percy said.

"They didn't have no stores to go to?" TJ asked.

"Of course not. You dumbass. Don't you know history?" Jake said.

"Ah know it well enough to know they did they're huntin' with bow and arrow," TJ replied.

"All right, fellas, let's not get into a fight here. We're gonna be workin' with guns, you know, on that huntin' expedition," Randy said.

"Ah don't think there is such a thing as a responsible gun owner, but ah'm not worryin' 'bout any of us shootin' each other," Percy said as the others laughed in unison.

"I've thought of something we could talk about," Randy said as he tried to redirect the conversation. "What do you think about the future of currency?"

"Ah've heard that in the future, everyone will have cards instead of cash, and anyone with cash will be looked upon as a criminal," TJ said.

"Ah've also heard in the future there will be security guards in supermarkets so that people won't be stealing food," Jake said.

"You've been listening to that crazy guy down the street again, haven't you?" TJ said.

"You mean, Frederick Jackson?" Jake replied.

"Isn't he the one that keeps talking about the end of the world?" Randy said.

"Yeah, but he knows a lot of things. He was a friend to some generals and colonels from what ah've heard."

"How did this conversation git to that crazy old hermit?" Randy asked.

"Well, it's better than talkin' about bitcoin," Percy said.

"Hey, I think bitcoin is the wave of the future. I've invested in it," Randy said.

"Bitcoin is not what you think it is. It's probably just some sham currency created by an international financier from Europe," Jake said.

"Well, I studied up on it, and I think it's the wave of the future," Randy replied.

"I do my tradin' with greenbacks. It's always worked for me. I don't know why anyone would want to walk around with a bunch of big ol' coins in their pockets," Percy said.

"It doesn't work that way. It's awl on the computer," Randy replied.

"Well, you're the only one who has a computer. The rest of us don't," Percy said.

"If you want to make it in this day and age, you have to keep up with the times. An' that means getting a computer or at least a smartphone," Randy said.

"Ah thank awl of us jus' have cell phones and are content with that," Percy said.

"Well, good for yew. Ah jus' lak keepin' up with the times," Randy said curtly.

They finished their biscuits after much discussion of their somewhat-planned itinerary for the weekend. They decided they weren't going to do any hunting the first night, just hiking and exploring. It was the second night that they decided they would try their hand at hunting quail and rabbit. Randy bragged about hunting wild boar with a bow and arrow, but the others weren't convinced that he had done much of that.

When they all got up to leave, they decided they would all convene at Randy's place around three in the afternoon. They would have time to do their exploring and hikin'. Percy's father was a forager, and Perry knew a little bit about it and was hoping to show the others his foraging skills. He knew Randy looked down on things like that, but he was hoping to spark the others' interest.

* * *

It was early in the morning, two weeks later, that the hard-liners met for their eggs and biscuits. They were all talking and bragging about the quail and rabbit they caught and a hidden clearing they had found in the woods.

"You know there's no telling what that clearin' originally was," Percy said.

"It could have been something for a witch's coven. You just never know," Jake queried.

"There's been stories about witches up in the mountains near here. I bet we could find a cave with things in it," TJ said.

"Most likely, it's probably some hermit's cave, not a witch's," Randy said.

"You never were a believer in the supernatural," Jake said to Randy.

"All that stuff is just make-believe. You'll never convince me you can detect ghosts in houses with their leftover electrical forces. All that is just to give people a reason to celebrate Halloween," Randy said. "There's a lot of money in the Halloween holiday."

"The problem with you, Randy, is you're too much of a non-believer. You think the world revolves around money and don't take solace in life's mysteries and wonders," TJ said.

"Take solace in life's mysteries and wonders? What do you think I am? Some kind of monk?" Randy mockingly replied.

"You certainly aren't anything like that," Percy answered.

"Well, none of us here are what you call monks," Jake said. "We've awl probably had trouble with the law at one time or another."

"I'll testify to that. I remember ma probation officer deliberately being a smart aleck to me. He said, 'Well, I guess we'll see you back here in a couple of years, won't we?'" TJ said.

"That's wut they do. They deliberately get you angry at them so that you do something wrong, and they can git you back in," Jake said.

"That's the way the system works. It's like a vacuum cleaner. I don't like a messy carpet. It's all about law and order. They have to do that," Randy said.

"So you're all for the military-industrial complex?" Percy asked.

"It's not a matter of the military-industrial complex. It's just a matter of keeping a clean house," Randy answered.

Percy was silent but eventually nodded his head in approval.

As they ate their biscuits, the waitress came over and offered more coffee. She was beginning to develop the habit of overhearing the men's conversations and joining in.

"You know, if it wouldn't for the owning of guns, I don't think America would have gotten as far as it did. Just think of all the farms saved because of them," Jake said. "Not to mention the collectibles," Jake added.

"They—! What about the women you protected?" Kay said.

"Women are only a necessary evil," Jake said.

"Well, maybe we are evil in our ways, but most men can't deal with the loneliness without them," Kay replied.

"Well, we're here to argue politics, not the importance of women in our lives," Randy said.

Kay looked offended and walked away in a huff.

"This brings me to something I've been wanting to talk about with you all. I think we should have a name for our group," Randy said.

"I've thought of that too. How's about the Biscuit-Eaters?" Jake said.

"I was thinkin' the Small Gamers," TJ said.

"How about The Hard-liners?" Percy said.

"That would explain our way of politickin', I would think," Jake said.

"So you're sayin' when it comes to taking a political viewpoint, we take the hard-line?" Randy asked.

"I would think so," Percy answered.

"Well, jus' because we got guns and are against the government doesn't mean we can't be more active in our politickin'," Jake said.

"I'm not big on all that activism, but I don't understand why hard-liners like us can't do something, like protest," Percy said.

"What would we be protestin'?" Jake asked.

"I don't know. Maybe protestin' the fact that we don't get to protest," TJ said.

"Well, let's get together and go down to the courthouse square and protest the fact that we don't get to protest," TJ said.

"Guys, I'm not too big on doing this. I'm going to have to be counted out," Randy said.

"Well, if you want to protest something else, that's fine," TJ said.

"Well, how's about tradition, family, and property as our line of protest? We could get some wood and cardboard and make the signs," Randy said.

With that thought, the four decided to call themselves The Hard-liners and meet at Randy's man cave to discuss how they were going to do their protest. They had decided on Randy's line of protest with signs that read, "Tradition, Family, and Property" and "Fishing teaches patience." They would conduct the protest the next Friday afternoon in the courtyard garden that accompanied the property of the courthouse.

* * *

On the day of the protest, all four of the hard-liners had sandwiches with them that their wives had made and decided to take breaks sitting on the garden wall in between periods of protest. Intermittent shouts were heard among them as they continued their prideful display in the cold winter air.

Some people began to form around the courtyard, watching with amusement at the four as they did their protestin' and politickin', but the hard-liners were unswayed by the small crowd and kept up their protest well into the afternoon. Some members of the crowd were confused by what the four were doing, but no one uttered a disrespectful shout or challenge to the hard-liners. As the afternoon ended, the hard-liners packed their lunchboxes and threw their signs into a local dumpster and headed back to their warm, modest homes on the outskirts of town.

The Dripping Faucet

Jerry was transfixed by the images on the screen. It was a superhero flick with a great deal of comedy in it. At points, Jerry was hysterical with laughter at the various satire in the film but seemed to be the only one in the theater that was laughing as much as he was. When he finished his popcorn, he debated whether he should skip some of the film and get another snack but decided he was too interested in the film and stifled his cravings.

Near the end of the film, the woman that sat in front of him decided to put on her flower hat that blocked the view of the screen. He looked to either side of the flower hat, trying to get a clear view of the movie and decided the best thing to do would be to move to another seat. He looked around and noticed on either side of him were empty seats with popcorn snacks occupying their closed positions. The owners of the popcorn on both sides were kids, and Jerry did his best to convince them to give up the seats with popcorn in them. The kids looked at each other and laughed and continued to watch the movie. Eventually, Jerry decided to move to the only seat in the back of the theatre and took in the remainder of the flick.

As he exited the theatre, he found his Toyota Corolla in the parking lot with no problem as he always made a mental note of where he was parked. When he entered his car, he was a little worried about getting the engine turned over since it was a fifteen-year-old model and probably needed repair, but it started up with very little of a problem, and Jerry was able to get to his apartment.

It was a brick stone apartment on the third floor that he lived in, and he was dissatisfied with his situation there. The cable was always going out at a hint of bad weather, and more importantly, he had a problem with a faucet that continuously dripped water. Sleeping became a problem, and Jerry was a nervous wreck as it was anyway.

He looked into his refrigerator and saw that he had only ramen noodles and some cheap tea to drink. He walked over to his radio and turned on the rock station. He was getting used to the redundancy of songs that it had to offer but had developed such a habit of listening to it. He didn't know what else to do. He didn't know how to shut it off.

The heavy emotions of the music began to make him more and more anxious as he listened to it. He began to dwell on the emotions, and a nervousness arose in him. He thought of the artist that was playing and all the no. 1 hits he had, and a tightness in his chest began to form. He felt excited about the artist and his success, and this continued to lead to his anxiety. The music seemed to give him a feeling of power, but he only wished that the next song wouldn't create this type of anxiety in him.

He walked back over to his refrigerator and took out his ramen noodles and began to focus on his supper for the night. Since his outing from the factory that was making management changes, he had to figure out a way to cut down on his expenses. To the landlord, "business was business," and he knew he could rely on his savings for a little while, but eventually, unemployment was going to run out, and he would have to get another job. He didn't worry about it too much. There seemed to be a lot of offers for jobs on his smartphone, and he was told this was good economic times.

As he was eating his ramen noodles, his smartphone began to vibrate. He picked up the phone and heard his ex-wife speaking to him even before he had a chance to speak to her.

"When are you gonna come by and take Charly?"

"I thought it was your turn," Jerry said.

"You're slipping, Jerry. I may have to tell my lawyer about you. The judge wouldn't look too kindly on it either."

"I guess I'll try to be over there as quick as I can."

Shayna was his ex-wife's name, and from the beginning, he felt he hadn't really gotten a fair deal in the divorce proceedings by the judge. He knew it would be a death sentence to argue about it, but he didn't understand why he had to end up helping her with various errands throughout the week. He was happy to do it but a little frustrated at times. He knew he had to share some of the responsibilities but felt it was a drag on his own personal time.

He knew his wife needed a docile person to do his bidding, and he didn't turn out to be that type of person. He was a mild-mannered enough person but decided the marriage game was over for him. The fruits of love and marriage had over-ripened, and the taste was not so sweet anymore.

He made his way in his beaten-up Toyota Corolla to his wife's apartment and knocked on the door, hoping Charly would answer it first. He was three years old and had answered it before as he was tall enough to reach the doorknob, but unfortunately, Shayna answered instead.

"Have you got any good news for me, or are you still bumming around for a job?"

"I probably got a job at a distribution plant for $15 an hour, but I don't know if I'll like it or not."

"Well, you better take it if you want to continue to see Charly." Charly was standing behind her, peeking around her skirt at Jerry.

Jerry smiled at Charly, and Charly smiled back. He was trying to develop some close attachment to Charly, but Shayna always seemed to be in between them, widening the distance between the two. He got down on his haunches and beckoned to Charly.

"Come on over here, Charly."

Charly smiled and walked from behind his mother's dress and put his arms around Jerry. Jerry hugged him back but couldn't help but feel a little disheartened by the situation. He knew Shayna was good at lobbying for better deals from the divorce settlement by furthering her education and getting more reputable employment than him.

"I'm going to take you to an amusement park today, Charly. We'll have lots of fun and cotton candy too."

Charly didn't understand all of what Jerry said but was happy anyways to hear him speak to him. Jerry picked him up and took him to his car after speaking to Shayna one last time.

"I'll have him back by nine," he said.

He put Charly in the driver's seat and heard in the distance Shayna cry out, "He needs a child's restraint seat."

"We'll be all right," Jerry replied.

The amusement park was just five blocks away from Shayna's apartment, and Jerry parked his car in a neighboring parking lot. The noise of the amusement park made him a little edgy, but he knew he could show Charlie a good time. At least he could get him on the merry-go-round and the Ferris wheel.

He nervously looked around for policemen, worrying about the overdue tags on his car. He hoped he could gather up the money to pay his tags soon and was taking a chance by spending the money on Charly and the amusement park instead but was sure he would be all right.

After about nine, he walked Charly back to his car and was relieved to see no citation on it. He hoped Shayna wouldn't raise a fuss about him bringing Charly home a little late like she used to raise a fuss about his cleanliness and bad habits. It always ended up making him feel unclean and unworthy. He remembered how she used to order him around to get things for her. He was glad that was over with.

As he drove up to her apartment, he saw that the light was still on. He took Charly to the front door and rang the bell. A little time passed before Shayna answered the door.

"You're a little late, but I'll let it pass this time."

Charlie held his hands out to his mother, and she picked him up and caressed his hair, and Jerry retorted, "I didn't buy him any beers this time."

Shayna gave a disgusted look on her face and led Charly in and closed the door.

"Can't even have a sense of humor around her," Jerry mumbled.

"I heard that," Shayna said through the door.

Jerry made his way home and noticed he hadn't grabbed the mail for the day. There was a letter from the cable company, which was probably a bill even though he hadn't been getting service for the last couple of weeks, and no technician bothered to stop by.

He went to his refrigerator and got some ramen noodles for the night and started thinking of Charly. He hoped he could get a better job than what he had so that he could set a good example for Charly. He knew he was not as computer savvy as Shayna was, but maybe he could get something that would make Charly proud of him.

He finished his meal of noodles and picked up his smartphone to look at some of the job offers in his email. He was glad he had several choices to make but wondered whether a lot of these offers were on the level or not. He remembered his mother saying, "Someday, these companies are going to be begging people for work." He felt that day might be here now. If he could get a couple of appointments with some employers, he might just land some kind of job.

After going through some of the offers on his smartphone, he decided he had enough of fiddling with it and turned on his radio instead. He turned it to the talk radio station and began listening to a conservative speaker that he listened to on occasion.

"America is at risk of losing all its economic credentials! We're beginning to become like the Roman empire! Or maybe like France after the French revolution when they owed all types of money to other nations! Other nations owe us money, but do we ask for it? Hell no! But these other countries that we owe money to may start getting itchy fingers and demand that money or else!" the speaker said.

"Folks, our economic system has become America's new tar baby! How are we going to dig ourselves out of this hole? Our morals and entertainment have reached the point of indecency! Have you ever looked at some of the new programs the big three networks have to offer us? They're trash! And it's all because of the degradation of our morals started by the looney left!" the speaker continued.

SURVEYS AND SCAMS

Jerry listened to the speaker and tried to decide if he was inciting hatred in his listeners or outlining what he felt were the country's problems. The speaker was somewhat of a celebrity from his national radio program, and he agreed with what he said a lot, but he didn't want to get consumed with hatred with what the speaker said.

He turned the radio off and sat alone in the darkness, thinking about what job opportunities might be in the local newspaper. He didn't subscribe to one but knew he could always go down to the shopping center in town and get a copy out of a machine. Boredom seemed to be the main reason for a lot of his actions, and he decided to leave the excruciating dullness of the house and get some kind of late-night snack at the local McDonald's and pick up a paper. He remembered there being a newspaper machine there as well.

He started his car up and began to make his way to McDonald's. It was late at night, but they were open, and luckily, it wasn't too late where he could dine inside. He would rather do that than have to grope for his wallet in the car in the drive-through. He parked his car and walked across the parking lot to the entrance. He looked around him at the high school kids in their cars and trucks cruising around late at night. He remembered himself doing the same thing a couple of years back.

As soon as he made the entrance, the door opened, and a bossy wife with her two children and obedient husband came out. Jerry let them pass and entered the restaurant. He decided to go to the kiosks instead of ordering from the clerk. He wanted to keep a low profile in this town and not make his presence known by the local government. He felt he had enough problems without having to deal with more.

He didn't have long to wait for his dollar meal, and he sat down at a chair near a window. He ate his double cheeseburger and looked at the kids in their jeeps and late-night trucks. It wasn't even homecoming, and they were out celebrating. That's all some kids seem to do—celebrate.

He took his fast-food garbage to the garbage can and looked around for late-night cops at the same time. After feeling a little more comfortable, he zipped up his jacket and walked out to his car. He started his engine, and it turned over, which was good enough for him and drove out of the parking lot dodging the jeeps and trucks of the privileged.

All he had to do was drive six blocks to his apartment, and maybe he could get home and get a good night's sleep. By the fifth block, he saw his apartment in the distance when he happened to look in his rearview mirror at the flashing lights of a police car. A feeling of despair came over him, and he pulled over his car to the side of the road.

He sat and waited while the policeman took his time and wrote the ticket in his police car. It was always an excruciatingly long time that Jerry had to wait for the policeman to come to his window and talk to him. He knew it was about his overdue tags and knew he was probably going to have to worry about a fine and court costs as well. Finally, the policeman walked up to his door and knocked on it.

"Do you realize you're driving with overdue tags?" the policeman said.

"I know, officer, and I'm willing to pay it, but things have come up that have caused my hands to be tied."

"Well, you better pay this by the date shown, or you will be in a heap of trouble."

"All right," Jerry said.

He didn't explain to the policeman that he had no idea how he was going to get the money by the date shown, but he knew better than to argue with the policeman.

As the policeman pulled away, Jerry started up his car again and made the final block to his apartment. He got out and hit his fist on the windshield in anger. After getting a ticket like this, he couldn't help but get a feeling of wanting to rebel against a policeman. This feeling of rebellion always rose up in him when something like this happened. He also began to realize there was no room for error in this new world. He walked into the house and lay down on the couch. As he sat there thinking, he could hear the drip, drip, drip of the dripping faucet.

The Clerk Job

James looked at the trees as he walked down the avenue of houses that led to the job he held at the local bookstore. He had already been there for two weeks and thought he was an avid reader who could hold down a job like this. The brown and green leaves were being blown by the wind on what was a fall day in the small town of Connecticut where James resided.

He reached the bookstore within fifteen minutes that he planned for himself and walked through the bell-ringing door. He didn't worry about having to answer to the owner tonight and made a safe smile to the clerk on duty. The clerk was a little perturbed at James as employees were told they had to show up at least fifteen minutes before their scheduled time, but James was confident she would give him some slack.

She was a pretty girl who seemed too young and unqualified for the job, but James thought he would give her some slack by not asking questions about books she had read. She looked up at the clock and looked at James with a sneering smile.

"I won't tell the owner this time, but you need to be here sooner. I've been on pins and needles, waiting for you so I can leave. I have a dance class to attend."

"Sorry about that," James said as he walked behind the counter to take her place.

"Maybe you could take some dance classes, James," the girl said in a taunting way. "I don't think you could pass the muster, but we could all have something to laugh at."

James knew he had to bite the bullet sometimes when dealing with coworkers at his job, so he passed off the comment and began to prepare for his job. He knew he had to deal with an uneven balance from the register from Mary, but he was prepared to make up the difference. Mary wasn't very good at basic math like he was.

James looked around the bookstore and decided since there weren't any customers around, he would work on some of the computer shipments. He made his way to the back room and saw three piles of books that looked like they needed to be shipped off. As he began to pack one of the boxes, he thought he heard whispering coming from the back door leading to the outside street.

He postponed packing to walk to the back door and search for the source of the whispering. He opened the back door but saw no one outside on the street. He returned to his packing and knew he had to use the computer to print the shipping labels. He was very nervous and anxious whenever he used the computer. For some reason, he was averse to computers and didn't like using them.

Working on the packing of another set of books, James felt an encroaching darkness begin to unfold into the backroom, and he had a nagging desire to close the door that led to the outside. He stared at the door for a second and then decided to walk over to the door and close it. He looked through the window at the dark and deserted street, thinking of the hardened criminals and perverts that could be roaming them and then put his hand on the window and pondered the thought for a while longer.

He eventually returned to the unshipped packages and resumed his duties to the bookstore. Suddenly, the bell to the front door of the shop rang, and James made his way to the front room. Standing in the doorway was an older man with a cane and spectacles. He was short and balding and had a foolish smile on his face.

"May I help you?" James said.

"I was wondering if you had any murder mysteries," the man said in a pert manner.

"Over by the magazines next to the romance section," James replied.

The man with the cane walked to the other end of the store while James looked at the register. He speculated why the man had decided to come into the store. Was he some kind of lookout for the bookstore's owner? Or maybe a spy from a rival bookstore? Or was he maybe a detective going undercover as a customer checking up on fraudulent activity in the town's stores?

James couldn't help but notice that the man looked a little like Truman Capote. He began to speculate about the possibility that Truman Capote was in the bookstore but was unsure if Truman Capote was even alive now. He thought it might be something to mention to his boss, but he wondered what his boss might think of him saying something like that.

Soon the man left, and James was all alone in the store again. It was growing dark, and again, he thought about lurkers and denizens outside of the store that might wish him harm. He knew the neighborhood was good, but he couldn't help but wonder about the dark motives and goals of average people in the community. He knew people had dark moods and thoughts and could follow through with them.

He grabbed a ruler sitting on the counter that he sometimes used to tap and hit the counter. It was a repetitious action that he engaged in to pass the time. It was a stress-reliever in a way too. He tried to hide it from the others at the bookstore, but he thought they probably knew about it.

He continued to tap the ruler incessantly on the counter, working things up in his mind and creating excitable feelings in his imagination. He knew eventually he would have to put a stop to this nervy, private act of his, but he was comfortable with it now and didn't try to curb his compulsion.

As the shift ended, James went to the door to lock it when he saw Elwin staring through the window at him. Elwin was another clerk at the bookstore that James had to get along with. He was a smart aleck who usually liked to bother James in some way. He stared through the window at James with a fixed expression on his face like a "you're a stupid person" stare. He pointed to the lock as if he was talking down to a child.

James opened it and let Elwin in.

"Are you always that stupid in figuring things out?" Elwin said. "I want to check on my schedule, dumbass." He walked behind the counter and looked at the paper schedule on the bulletin board in the back room. He was humming some song that he had on his iPod. He walked back to James and the front counter and blew a bubble in James's face.

"So how many customers did you get tonight?" Elwin said.

"Oh, just one guy that looked like Truman Capote."

"Who's Truman Capote?"

"He's just this author," James said.

"You know, you're not going to get very far in life being a bookworm. I guess we can expect that from a nerd like you."

Elwin walked out of the bookstore, leaving James behind the register. It was when he was alone that James's curiosity became aroused, and he decided to walk over to the book stacks and shelves to see what was being sold to the customers.

He looked at the romance section and picked a book from the shelf. He opened the book and noticed at the front all the accolades and positive reviews that were given for the book. He read some passages and decided the writing style was not for him. He walked over to the horror section and looked at the Lovecraft rip-offs and noticed similar accolades on the front and back covers.

He then walked over to the back room where the Christian books were sold. The room was poorly lit, but James noticed a small bookcase underneath a window situated in the back. He was unsure what kind of books were in this little bookcase, so he bent down and picked one up. It was a small book of poetry by some unknown poet. He flipped through the book and noticed no accolades or positive reviews in the book. He then noticed a book by Dickens called *Great Expectations*. He noticed it was an old edition of the book, and as he flipped through it, there was a note near the middle of the book that fell onto the floor. James reached down and picked up the piece of paper. Written on it were the words "Don't give up hope—you matter."

James was dumbfounded by the note and couldn't help but wonder if it was meant for him. At times, he would have thoughts about messages he felt were directed at him. He would hear broadcasters on television and think they were sending messages to him. He thought strangers on the street were talking to him with their minds. Now there was this message in a book at a place where he worked with a clear sign of loving concern directed at what might be him.

He took the paper and stuck it in his pocket. He then went back to the cashier's stand and waited for the owner to drop by for the night. The owner was not the most understanding of bosses he had encountered, but James felt comfortable working in a bookstore, and if he had to put up with some abuse, he would.

After a while, he decided to go to the backroom and sneak a snack from the refrigerator. He noticed two boxes that still hadn't been packed yet. He opened the refrigerator and took out a microwave dinner and set it in the microwave. He pressed the timer, wondering if the boss might catch him taking a food break like this.

When he began to take the food out of the microwave, he heard the front door's bell ring. He could tell it was his boss by the rhythm and space of his footsteps.

"James, I would like to have a word with you," the owner said.

James gulped down his food, realizing he had already broken the "food break rule" of the owner's as well as "who knows what else."

"I'm able to monitor store's video cameras with my smartphone, and I've noticed you have left your clerk post to browse the bookstore. This is a direct violation of my policies and rules for associates at my store. I am not pleased with your job performance and would like to hear what you have to say for yourself."

James swallowed hard and responded, "There was nobody in the store at the time, so I thought I would look around a little bit."

The owner gave James a cold stare. He then responded, "It's not your job to peruse the store for your own enjoyment. You can do that when you're not working. Now tell me why you're eating food when it's not your food break?"

"There were just a couple more boxes to pack, so I thought it would be no harm to take a short food break."

"Time is money. I won't report you this time on my log, but discipline is imminent."

The owner checked his watch with the clock on the wall and synchronized it so he could more effectively monitor his employees' time. He grabbed a box of doughnuts out of the refrigerator and took it with him as he left through the back door. James breathed a sigh of relief and thought about the remaining packages he had to send off for the night.

As he returned to the cash register, he looked outside at the deepening night. A dark veil of thoughts began to consume him, and the store seemed to grow shadows of its own. The shadows in the store loomed larger and larger, and he began to think about enemies and culprits wandering in the outside alleys and streets. His sight grew clouded with darker and darker visions of the night. His mind began to wander into thoughts of vandalism and violence.

He walked back into the back room and finished up the remaining packages that needed to be shipped. He executed as much self-control as he could in his work to be done for the night. He tried to ignore the whisperings that he heard near him and from the other rooms in the bookstore. The voices in his head would make their remarks and comments on his job performance. He did his best to ignore them. When he finished his work, he went back to the front of the store and waited for the end of his shift.

* * *

It was raining outside when James walked into the bookstore for what he decided would be his last shift. He had no idea what he would do after this but felt the voices in his head were telling him the right way. He felt there were far too many conspiracies to unravel and mysterious phenomena to discover than to spend his time brooding in a bookstore.

Waiting behind the register was Mary. As soon as she saw James, she bolted into the back room in her regular "high and mighty" way.

A second later, she returned with the owner, and he stared at James with the same contemptuous stare he always made to James.

"I've heard you want to quit your job here," the owner said.

"Where did you hear that?"

"You confided in someone you thought was your friend."

"Who?"

"Elwin."

"Well, I was going to tell you today."

"Well, I'm not going to give you a chance. You're fired."

James walked out of the bookstore as the owner and cashier, Mary, looked on with their arms folded and smug smiles on their faces.

As soon as James left the store, the sky began to clear up, and the sun came out. James passed the alleyway by the store when he heard a "pssst." He turned and saw a man in a suit waving to him with a friendly smile on his face. James walked back over to the alleyway as the man held out his hand to shake.

"Hello, James. You don't know who I am, but I'm with an organization that helps people like you. We call ourselves the OMD, the Organization of the Mentally Displaced. We travel around the country, looking for various victims of a society that exists in our midst. We feel you fit our qualifications and deserve special attention," the man in the suit said.

James shook his head and thought about what the man said. He wasn't overly skeptical of the man but had questions to ask him about his organization.

"How do you know my name?" James asked.

"We have been following you and your family for some time now and noticed the victimization of you and your family."

"How are you able to do these things?" James asked.

"We operate independently and have donors from various sects of society that help out with the funding of our operation. We wish to take you under our wing and treat you the way you deserve to be treated. Do you feel you have been mistreated?"

"I've never really thought about it. I've always thought that maybe I deserved it. I was doing something that was stupid and needed the discipline that I got," James said.

"Well, you didn't deserve the 'discipline,' James," the man said.

"You have talents and intelligence that can be cultivated, and we think we can help you with that."

"Are you going to charge my family money for this?"

"No charge."

"What all will I do in your organization?"

"We can get into the details later, but let me first tell you my name is Roberto, and I will be escorting you home to your residence."

The man took James by the hand and escorted him to a white van that had the organization's name on it. James was not afraid when he got into the front seat of the van, and for some reason, he had a strong trust in Roberto. In the back seat were other people that were complete strangers to James, but he felt oddly at home with them. Roberto started the van and drove through the street to transport the various occupants to their somber destinations.

Podunk Hill

It wasn't always this way. Chester was used to the derision and flak he used to receive from his buddies in the backwater country where he lived and worked, but he always felt there was something higher to attain somewhere else. It wasn't always this way though. He counted on his old friend Reginald to give him the proper advice on the manners and etiquette that the backwater country was so deficient in giving him.

Chester was big, and his height was measured at about 6'2". He had a disorganized growth of light brown hair and never seemed to have lost his baby fat. His friend Reginald was thin and about the same height as him, with more austere facial features and a shock of curly hair. He had darker skin, but Chester didn't let that bother him. He knew Reginald had the dibs on things that he felt were necessary for "the good life." Reginald was from the backwater country but was raised in what Chester felt was an upstanding background. Reginald did not have the obligatory motorbike on his porch, and the family had a bookcase of books.

Reginald prided himself and his family for their literacy and the selection of books they had. His father had the complete foxfire collection of Appalachian folklore and customs. He always felt it was needed as some kind of survivalist's handbook just in case there was a breakdown of civilization or massive power grid failure. Reginald's father was also a collector of history books and books on political discourse. Reginald himself was familiar with some of the classics like *Gulliver's Travels* and *The Adventures of Huckleberry Finn.*

Reginald was not good in a fight though. He also had bad eyes that never allowed him to do well in the local archery and marksmanship competitions. He was never considered a good hunter by any standards, so he ended up becoming a close confidante of Chester for his knowledge of politics and backwater folklore. He also was good at foraging the berries and nuts in the area, not to mention his knowledge of mushrooms and poisonous snakes.

Chester, on the other hand, was good in a fight and seemed to have a natural way with women that the others admired. He also knew how to clean and shoot a gun. This was considered impressive by the local group of backwater friends that Chester had. Reginald never quite fit in with these friends, but because of his father's education, he was respected in the area.

Both Reginald and Chester were sharing a pint of whisky one night, sitting on a picnic table talking up a storm. Chester wanted to talk to Reginald about current and future endeavors he may want to take in his life path, and he knew Reginald knew a lot about "life paths" with his knowledge of Indian folklore.

"What kind of life path are you trying to pursue?" Reginald tried to impress Chester with his question.

"I was thinking of something in politics and law," Chester said.

"That would take a lot of studyin' and knowledge in order to pursue such a craft," Reginald said.

"Do I really have to do all that readin'? I would like to just take in lectures and hands-on training. It's what I'm best at," Chester replied.

"There are only some rites of passage that you really have to go through in order to get 'the good life' if that's what you're really interested in," Reginald said.

"You mean some kind of hazing or something? I don't know if I want to get branded or not," Chester said.

"Well, if you have a low threshold on pain, you probably don't need to be thinking about doing these things," Reginald said.

"I'd like to have experiences like that so I can talk a lot of shit to girls. I run out of shit to talk to them about," Chester said.

"You usually seem to have your way with women. They realize you're a kind of leader of the pack," Reginald assured Chester.

"How should I conduct myself when I'm leadin' the pack?" Chester asked.

"Pick on the weak one. It'll make you appear strong in front of the others," Reginald advised.

"You think so?" Chester wondered.

"According to my father, methods like that have always worked throughout history for leaders," Reginald said.

"That sounds like something to try on my local group. That's for sure," Chester said.

"It wouldn't hurt," Reginald replied.

Chester tugged on his overalls with his thumb. This was a nervous habit he had to help him think about things. He then reached into his deep side pocket and pulled out a can of chewing tobacco. He chewed for a little while and then spat a chunk of saliva at his feet. He wanted to impress Reginald by showing him he knew how to spit right. He figured that Reginald understood that a good leader is one who knows how to spit.

"What kind of chewing tobacco do you have?" Reginald said.

"Red Man," Chester answered enthusiastically.

"You need to switch to Beechnut. It's a much more high-profile chewing tobacco. It would impress the girls," Reginald said.

"I think I'm more interested in impressing the local buddies. They're the ones that will be my following, aren't they?" Chester said.

"Yeah, but you don't want to get stuck in a company of giggling women because you walk around with Red Man instead of Beechnut," Chester said.

Chester mulled this over for a while and scratched his head as if he didn't know what to do.

"You could always switch one for the other according to whatever social situation you're in," Reginald tried to save face with Chester with his comment.

"Usually, these guys stick to one type of chewing tobacco. I don't want to be two-faced."

"That's very commendable, but I don't think it would hurt to have some social skills," Reginald replied.

"I know I could be a good leader. I just know it," Chester said.

"Then mainly we need to talk about your hair."

"What's wrong with my hair?"

"It needs to be styled more. Any politician would tell you that."

"I can't be too concerned about my hair if I'm going to get to have ta prove myself in a lot of fights," Chester said.

"There are actually very few fights that you'll have to prove yourself in. The only thing you will really have to prove yourself for is being caretaker of Podunk Hill."

"Podunk Hill? What's that?"

"The proving ground for all things substantial. The testing place for all great leaders. The one and only location that substantiates your mettle with men and women. The haven of truth. The harbor of righteousness. The port of all things plenty."

"What is this place?" Chester said.

"It's a swimming hole south of these woods," Reginald said.

"Why is it called Podunk Hill?"

"The swimming hole where everyone congregates and parties is a draw in the hill we call Podunk Hill. It's a hill with no known property owner. Only the caretaker controls it."

"Who's the caretaker?"

"No one knows him personally. He just oversees the place. He's a big beer drinker himself. He has a big belly and wears one of those chains connecting his wallet to his pants."

"How come no one knows him personally?"

"That's just the way he is. Being the caretaker, he does let us bring all types of beer and pot to the place. He doesn't let us make a big mess there though. That's why he's the caretaker."

"What's so big about being a caretaker of this place?"

"Lots of important people have come to Podunk Hill to party and talk about things. You know. Philosophy and such. The caretaker ends up being the one who steers the conversation in the direction he wants. He also gets to make decisions about certain things."

"Like what?"

"Well, like how long the drinking party should go on? Whose job is it to stash the pot and liquor? You know when you're the caretaker, you can delegate authority."

"I've never delegated authority before. I'd like to try that," Chester said.

"So you would like to be the caretaker of Podunk Hill? It is a leadership role that probably involves some book-learnin' in my dad's history books. Are you up for it?" Reginald asked.

"I think so."

"There's also a test known as the test of mettle," Reginald said.

"I was afraid of that. What does that involve?"

"Walkin' on a rope bridge. Seein' how's much pain you can take. And most important, the contest of wills with the caretaker himself," Reginald said.

"You mean I have to fight the caretaker?" Chester asked.

"If'n you want to be caretaker yourself. It's the only way."

"Aw'll have to think about this. Maybe I could talk to my friends about this."

"You have to show tolerance too. That's jus' what leaders have to do now. It might be a good idea to meet with your friends," Reginald said.

"Should I tell them I want to be caretaker of Podunk Hill?" Chester asked.

"I wouldn't discuss any political ambitions to any of them," Reginald said.

"Well, on that note, ah think I'll go home to my weight set and do some repetitions before the sun goes down," Chester said.

"Let me know when you want to meet with your friends so's I can show you how to use the leadership skills that I've taught you on them," Reginald said.

The birds were still chirping as the day came to an end, and the clouds gathered into gray rainclouds that would surely lead to rain for the night and possibly the next day. Chester seemed unconcerned about the rain as he got into his jeep and left for home. Reginald pulled up his jacket and hood as he always knew how to dress for the weather and got on his motorbike and went back to his dad's house where he lived.

"I don't know how I'm going to act to them when we congregate for the political meetin'," Chester said.

He was sitting at the small dining room table that Reginald had at his father's place. Chester meant to ask him what happened to his mother, but he never mustered up the courage to say it. He knew his father worked at the local factory and liked to dictate to his son various political writings and essays that he read. Chester decided Reginald might be very touchy about his mother, so he wanted to keep the conversations to be mainly about politickin' instead.

"I would keep your ambitions about Podunk Hill under wraps. They ain't needin' to know about you or Podunk Hill," Reginald said.

"Do you think any of them know about Podunk Hill?"

"Probably not. Nevertheless, I'd keep it secret from them. You don't need any more competition for a caretaker."

"I'm not always getting a hard time from those guys. Sometimes, they say things that make sense. What's important is the male power structure I'm dealin' with. These guys know the ins and outs of political dealin's in this area. They also work at some of the better factories 'round here. I know that makes a difference," Chester said.

"Well, I still think you need to keep Podunk Hill a secret. It'll be like a political bargaining block you have over them," Reginald said.

"Ah think those guys will think differently about me if'n I was to become caretaker," Chester said.

"Well, let's not put the cart before the horse. We'll get a few beers and meet out at the lake. Then you can use a few of the leadership skills I've taught you on them," Reginald said.

"So what's for supper?" Chester asked.

"I think my dad has caught some catfish for us. I'll put some on the grill, and we'll read from one of my dad's history books."

"Remember, you were going to teach me chess too," Chester said.

"We'll get to that soon enough. Let's have that catfish."

* * *

Reginald was clearing the dinner table when Chester went over to their dinner cabinet and got the chess set. Chester began to set up the chess game as he knew how from Reginald. He remained perplexed about the whole game but felt it was some necessary thing he had to learn.

Reginald didn't seem to have a difficult time explaining to Chester how all the pieces moved until they came to the knight. Chester was challenged by how the piece moved. Eventually, after an hour or two, he figured it out. When he learned how to checkmate, he began to realize what he felt was the importance of chess.

"I think I know the meaning of power now," Chester said.

"Well, don't let it go to your head. When we meet with your friends tomorrow night at the regional park site, you're going to have to be playing a good leadership role in order for them to be some kind of followers," Reginald replied.

"I can do it. I just know I can."

They carefully put up the chess set and put it back in Reginald's cabinet, and Chester handed Reginald the phone numbers of his back country friends.

"I'll make all the arrangements so you can study those history books I gave you," Reginald said.

Chester gave Reginald a curt salute and put Reginald's history books in his backpack and got into his jeep to head for home. They both were a little nervous about the whole affair with Chester's back country friends tomorrow but were also excited and enthused as well. The jeep drove off as the summer sun began to fall, and the day got cooler. Reginald secretly wished for another leader than the one he was grooming as he watched the jeep drive out of his yard.

* * *

Reginald and Chester were sitting at a picnic table when they saw Bart and his friends drive into the regional park on his pickup truck. Bart was a bearded, overweight man with a group of followers of his own who piled into his pickup truck: one riding shotgun while the other two riding in the back. The day was clear, so no one worried about getting rained on.

Jacob (the shotgun rider) was Bart's right-hand man who knew a lot about fixing up things like cars and electronics. They pretty much told the others what to do, and Chester didn't even remember the names of the others, and as the fifth one came up the road on his motorbike, Chester ignored him and cast all his attention on Bart and Jacob.

"What did you ask us over here for? You better be glad it didn't rain today, or I would have tied you up in all sorts of knots," Bart threatened.

"We feel we would like to use you all as sounding boards for some of our ideas," Chester said timidly.

Bart's group laughed.

"Sounding board? I'm no damn sounding board!" Bart exclaimed. "We don't want to be a part of no damn political discussion."

"It's more than a political discussion. It's more like a political exercise," Reginald said.

"Well, we're not doing any push-ups or two-mile run. We're here to hang out. What exactly are you talking about when you say political exercise?" Bart asked.

"Some kind of activity maybe to test your political wits and knowledge. A game possibly of skill and proficiency in the political arts. A political exercise," Reginald said.

"That sounds like too much work. We came here to relax. Jacob is going to tell us some stories, but if you got something more interesting to do, we might be on board," Bart said.

"Well, I'm going to try to make this political exercise like what they had one time at this gaming convention I went to in Atlanta. It was a test of wits and one's proficiency in a real-time political situation. How would you handle it? You know? It was done electronically, but I could cook something up that we could do here," Reginald said.

SURVEYS AND SCAMS

"You know, sort of like Kennedy and the Cuban missile crisis. How would you have responded, y' know?"

"I think I might be able to do something like that. C'mon, guys, let's all gather around the tables here an' see what this is all about."

The six men gathered around the picnic tables as Reginald and Chester stood standing as they tried to direct the others in a way that was suitable to their game. Bart took out some trail mix and handed one to Jacob. The others were talking among each other when Reginald signaled to Bart to quiet things down.

"All right, you all shut up while these guys conduct this political exercise!" Bart shouted.

The others looked around in disgust as Reginald began.

"First, I want to see how up you are in political correctness. First of all, how would you respond to a good-looking female secretary in a short skirt coming to your office taking notes?"

"Well, being a big politician, I'd probably try to hit on her a little just to spice things up," Bart said.

"Incorrect. You can't do things like that if you want to be a good politician. No matter how honest you may be, it's not allowed in the political arena these days. Another question. What if you have been noticing a somewhat friendly power conducting treachery against your country by allying and supporting a known enemy of yours?" Reginald asked.

"Well, I would want to kick their ass the first chance I got," Bart said.

"That would be the wrong thing to do. This is a friendly power, and no matter how treacherous they are, you have to be nice to them. Finally, if in debates for the primaries you end up getting criticized ruthlessly by other members of your party, how should you treat them after the elections?"

"Well, I wouldn't want to be friends with them or have them on my side," Bart answered.

"Wrong again. You must be nice to them and treat them with acceptance and friendship."

"This sounds like a lot of bullshit I don't want to get involved in. Count me out of politics. C'mon, fellas, let's get out of here." Bart gestured to the others as they all rose up from the picnic table and made their way back to his pickup truck.

Chester looked at Reginald with a puzzled expression. He wasn't sure what to think of Bart's response to the political exercise. Chester scratched his head and started to clean up some of the mess Bart's gang left on the picnic table.

"Well, that's a political exercise I think anyone would have to take in order to test their political proficiency," Reginald said.

"After hearing all that, I'm not sure if I can handle politickin' too well," Chester said.

"Well, don't worry about it too much. If you can become caretaker of Podunk Hill, that will solve a lot of your problems."

"You think I will have it in the sack?"

"Pretty much. Podunk Hill is known for its political influence on the rich, party-going youth of the area. You'll have everything in the bag, so to say," Reginald said.

"So what is it I have to do again?"

"Just show the current caretaker who's boss of Podunk Hill."

"Will I have to maybe get into a fight with him?"

"It's possible."

"Is the caretaker a big guy?" Chester asked.

"Oh yeah, but you're big too, so I think you can handle him," Reginald said.

"do you know where this place is?" Chester said.

"I think I know a time when we can drive up there and meet the caretaker. Would you like a contest with him? Maybe next Friday?" Reginald asked.

"I don't know. That's kind of sudden."

"The more you hold it off, the more afraid you'll get of it," Reginald quipped.

With a groan, Chester agreed, and they both headed back to their vehicles. They left the park with a roar of their engines.

* * *

The day of Thursday was an uneventful one, and Chester visited Reginald at his house to get the details of the contest. Chester walked into the room and saw Reginald at the dining room table with some items laid out before him. There were some brass knuckles, some kind of manual, and what looked like a bottle of pills.

"What is this?"

"Just some tools of the trade. The brass knuckles are for the fight, the manual is social etiquette, and the pills are energy boosters. I feel these are three things you're going to need in your future as leader of Podunk Hill. Now you're going to have to meet the caretaker Friday morning, so it's going to be a little foggy. The leader of Podunk Hill is what you would call a 'good ole boy.' We live in a good ole boy system in these parts, so you're going to have to learn to be one as well," Reginald said.

"Ah think I know how to be a good ole boy. I've got the size and the political know-how. Ah have jus' one question. Why Friday morning?" Chester asked.

"It's the mornin' before the weekend, and we git some partygoers up on Podunk Hill. Campers, drinkers, and such. They're all there for a good time at the swimmin' hole," Reginald said.

"This fog that you talk about. Will it keep us from findin' the place?" Chester asked.

"Ah know these roads well enough to find it in the fog," Reginald said.

"Well, ah've been able to handle Bart on occasion, so ah think ah kin' handle this caretaker of yours," Chester said.

"I'll pick you up around four tomorrow so we can get a head start on things," Reginald said as Chester began to leave.

Reginald called out to Chester to get the items on the table, and Chester winced a little as he picked them up.

He left Reginald's house in his jeep to make an early night of it. Reginald watched him leave, still doubting the whole situation he had with Chester.

* * *

"Make a right here," Reginald said to Chester in his jeep in the early morning as they made their way through the twisting and winding roads of the back country. Chester had hunted in these areas, but it was Reginald who knew the roads best.

The jeep started to climb a hill, and Chester came to the realization that this must be Podunk Hill. Reginald continued to steer Chester in the right direction and eventually found a parking space for the jeep.

"The swimming hole is right up the road there." Reginald pointed to the trail on Chester's right. It was about four thirty in the morning, and Reginald thought the caretaker would be waiting there, preparing for the festivities of Friday night.

"I hope these brass knuckles will come in handy. Ah've already taken two pills, but ah don't think that book is goin' to help me at all," Chester said.

"I think they will help your situation more," Reginald said.

Reginald looked at Chester and put his hand on his shoulder. "Now's the time to prove yourself. Good luck and Godspeed."

Chester gave Reginald a critical look as he climbed out of the driver's side of the jeep and started to walk down the trail to Podunk Hill.

* * *

The fog was still resting on the road and nearby forest as Chester made his way to the clearing where the swimming hole was supposed to be. It wasn't until the hole was in sight behind a clump of trees that Chester realized how much the fog was laying. He put his brass knuckles on and swallowed two more pills. He then walked between two trees and took a good look around at the swimming hole.

At this early in the morning, the fog covered most of the water and some of the trees on the other side of the water. The whole scene had an otherworldly quality to it. The vision felt fey in Chester's mind. He caught a fleeting glimpse in his vision but turned to look in the direction of the object to find nothing.

SURVEYS AND SCAMS

In the distance, Chester saw a lone figure in between a clump of trees shrouded by the fog. As the fog moved away from the large silhouette, Chester could make out who it was.

It was Bart!

Chester froze up and stood transfixed by the image of Bart and realized who he had to vie for caretaker of Podunk Hill. Bart was the caretaker!

He began to see Bart tilt his head to one side with a puzzling and then bellowed out, "If you've come this early to this swimming hole, you must be tryin' to make some kind of power play!"

Chester's knees almost buckled, but he held his ground and made his reply.

"I'm the rightful caretaker of Podunk Hill, and I intend to prove it."

"If you think you can rightfully enter the good ole boy system, then bring it on, young lad!"

Chester crouched down like a sumo wrestler as he stood and faced Bart. Both had their arms raised in a wrestling stance and began to circle around each other, waiting for an opportunity to attack. Bart would throw out his arm every so often, taunting Chester to strike in some way. After a couple of feints and false blows, Chester grabbed Bart's neck and tried to get him into a headlock. At first, he succeeded and held Bart down. He knew Bart was a good deal older than him, and he could maybe beat him with his endurance, but Bart had tricks of his own.

As Chester held Bart below him, Bart reached up with his right hand and used his fingers to press on one of Chester's eyes.

"Ow!" Chester said as he loosened his grip on Bart.

Bart wrestled his way out of the headlock and got back on his feet again to lay a heavy blow to Chester's left ear. Chester had pocketed his brass knuckles but felt it might be time to put them back on again. He thought the fighting was getting a little dirty, and he had to equal up the contest with his brass knuckles. He stepped back after the blow to the ear to reach into his pocket for the brass knuckles, but Bart was unto him and charged him into the ground as the brass knuckles went flying out of Chester's hands.

They wrestled on the ground for a minute or so until Chester grabbed hold of Bart's pinky finger and bent it back against the outside of his hand. Bart let out a yell, "Not my pinky finger, not my pinky finger. I'll do whatever you say."

Chester got on his feet, and Bart remained sitting, holding his finger with pain. Chester realized he had found Bart's weak spot pretty quickly.

"Am I going to get some kind of agreement from you on who should be the caretaker of this place?" Chester said.

"I don't know yet. I've got to think about this," Bart said.

"I could always go for your groin—"

"That's all right. You've got me. You've got me. If you feel you kin' run this place better than me, you kin' have the full caretakin' duties. I'm finished here," Bart said.

Bart got on his knees and then on his feet and began to walk down to the shed behind the trees. He opened the door of the shed and went in and then came back out with the keys to the shed. He handed them to Chester and walked with a dejected look to the trail that Chester assumed led to his pickup truck.

"How come I didn't know it was you?" Chester asked as Bart was walking away.

"You'll have to talk about that with Reginald," Bart said as he walked away to his pickup truck.

Chester looked around at his new domain. The otherworldly vision he had earlier was fading away as the fog disappeared with the early morning. He looked at the swimming hole full of beer cans and ashtrays made out of the small depressions in the rocks. He wasn't sure if he was interested in the cleanup of this place, but that thought disappeared when he realized he would be sharing time with high-profile rich kids wanting to party at this famous well-known place.

Motivated by this thought, he started to walk back to his jeep when he saw Reginald walking up the road toward him. Immediately, he had a lot of questions he wanted to ask Reginald but realized one remained the most in his mind.

"Why didn't you tell me the caretaker was Bart?"

"I didn't want you to chicken out if you knew it was him," Reginald said.

"Well, it's been done. I'm the leader of Podunk Hill now. When do I start leading the flock?"

"The flock is led best by the wisdom of the shepherd," Reginald said.

"With that in mind, I think I'll go home and read your book on social etiquette. It should get me off to a good start."

Reginald gave Chester a good ole boy slap on the shoulder as Chester walked back to his jeep with dreams of political leadership dancing in his head.

Apotheosis

It was two in the morning when Gilbert and Zak exited the movie theater called *The Movie Zone*. It was a whole night of movie features that they watched, and they were somewhat glad that it finally ended. The movies were on the lower end of the scale of movies to be watched, but they enjoyed joking about them in the theater and afterward when they had a chance to talk about them.

Gilbert and Zak had known each other for a length of about two years. They had lived in the city since their college years and were both a part of the new wave/goth scene for some time. They both had attended the same college, but Gilbert was older than Zak, and they had attended college at different times.

They met two years back when they discovered they had similar interests in music and movies. Gilbert liked sports while Zak was into science fiction, but they both were comfortable being the "straight" friends that they were and would go to places having fun with their commentaries of movies and music.

As they walked down the city streets, Gilbert pulled his jacket around him for protection from the cold night air. It was the beginning of fall, so neither of them had dressed in anything heavy for the night. Gilbert, the bigger guy, usually walked Zak to his apartment before going back to his place with his mother. They both had jobs at odd shifts, so they had to work around their schedules to hit the clubs when they wanted to. As Zak's apartment came into sight, Gilbert waved goodbye to Zak and made his way home to his mother.

The next weekend night, Gilbert and Zak waited in line at a club called the New Wave Enclave. Both still had their hairstyles from the '80s and liked this club because of the old songs they remembered when they were young. The line was not too long, and it gave Gilbert and Zak a chance to scout out the place and the people that were going to be there that night.

They whispered jokingly to themselves about some of the other's hairstyles. Zak noticed one guy who had an outfit like Dexy's Midnight Runners. He mentioned it to Gilbert, and Gilbert smiled and said in a low tone to Zak, "I have no idea how he is going to dance tonight. I hope it's not too energetic of a dance where he takes up the whole floor."

As they walked into the dark-lit club with its pounding drumbeat and crowded bar, they noticed a booth with two empty seats on one side and two girls on the other side of the booth. One girl had a gothic-style hairdo with curls that came over one side of her face, and the other girl had green hair. They both sat on one side of the booth, seemingly inviting anyone to sit on the other side.

Gilbert whispered to Zak what he thought was an opening from the two girls, and Zak agreed. They both went to the booth, and Gilbert gestured to the girls to be seated, and they agreed with hand gestures of their own to sit in the booth.

Gilbert and Zak piled into the other side of the booth and took complimentary breadsticks that were placed on the table by a waitress. Both girls looked at each other and laughed as Gilbert began to cough on his breadstick.

"You girls are different than a lot of the other girls in this place," Zak decided to start the conversation.

"We believe in opening social lines for the opposite sex rather than hiding in social groups and clicks like the others," the one with the green hairstyle said.

"Well, I guess we need to introduce ourselves. I'm Gilbert, and this is Zak," Gilbert said.

"I'm Shannon, and this is Rebecca," the girl with the green hairstyle gestured with her hand to her other friend.

"How's the music here?" Gilbert asked Shannon.

"It reminds me a lot of what I used to listen to when I was in college six years ago. I remember hearing some of these songs coming out of the college dorm room windows as I would walk to my class," Shannon said.

"Yeah, I remember a lot of these songs had interesting videos to them too," Gilbert added. "Mainly, it was new wave songs from Europe that I was interested in. I still have my hairstyle from those days."

"So I've noticed!" Shannon said, and Rebecca giggled.

"I was more interested in the goth scene myself," Zak said with his black tassel of hair hanging over his eyes. He also had the obligatory goth ring in his nose.

"The goths always liked to hang out in their own enclaves with each other, and there would always be maybe one certain club they would go to in college," Gilbert said in a critical tone.

"I remember that. I was kind of a goth myself," Shannon said.

"What do you think of this club?" Gilbert asked Shannon.

"I've been to better ones than this, but at least, they play the music that's more my type of music," Shannon replied.

"They don't have a disco ball on the dance floor, but I guess that's for just the gay bars now," Rebecca said as she threw back the tassel on her forehead.

"So what were your majors in college?" Shannon asked Gilbert.

"I was religious studies, and Zak was sociology," Gilbert said.

"Sociology? That sounds interesting. What were some of the things you learned in your classes?" Shannon asked.

"Well, for one thing, most people marry someone that is on the same income level as they are," Zak said.

"Shouldn't you marry someone you love?" Gilbert said.

"I guess they figure they will probably love each other enough or learn to love each other," Zak said.

"I was always interested in the new wave music from Europe. Is there anything sociological about that?" Gilbert said.

"You're not ethnocentric. You don't believe in just your own country's culture as entertainment. You look elsewhere. Some people only believe in buying and listening to things from their own country," Zak said.

"I always liked new wave songs from Europe better than the American music. I was never into Michael Jackson," Shannon said.

"American music tends to be not as interesting as European music," Rebecca said. "There's always the goth stuff, too, you know."

"What do your sociology classes talk about when it comes to economic issues, like socialism and capitalism?" Shannon asked.

"I think all my teachers and professors were socialists. You can pretty much tell that," Zak said.

"One social thing I've noticed is the type of people that look at you with suspicion when you act friendly to them. They immediately assume you want something from them. That's the sign of what I think is a hard-core capitalist," Gilbert said.

"I know the type of person you're talking about. I hate people like that," Shannon said.

"Those types of people, I think, are like Nazi SS officers," Gilbert mumbled.

"What other things have you noticed about our society?" Shannon said to Zak.

"Well, have you noticed there are types of people in our social order who always do what they're told and that's it?" Zak said. "They're also people who usually are without any kind of guile or wit if you've ever noticed."

"I think I know who you're talking about. They also tend to be disrespectful of intelligence. They don't like people they think who are 'too smart for their own good,'" Shannon said.

"You mean 'robo-humans?'" Gilbert said.

The other three gave forced laughs to this comment. They lowered their heads in resignation, and Zak tried to change the subject.

"I remember working in a pizzeria doing the dishes on the weekend when boys would come in with their girlfriends and go straight to the jukebox and play 'Black Dog' by Led Zeppelin just about every Friday and Saturday night. It's like they were flaunting their privileged status," Zak said.

"They probably got the big trucks they drive around in by their daddies when they turned eighteen and got some kind of job working in a factory for good pay because of their families' pull or influence in the town," Shannon said.

"They also got their hunting and fishing licenses when they were young too," Rebecca said.

"I never learned how to camp out or fish," Gilbert said. "I was never a Boy Scout either."

"It's no big deal. You learn a little about starting fires and selling cookies in the Girl Scouts, but I don't think I could survive in the wilderness," Shannon said.

"I was never interested in things like that. I always like watching football on television and listening to music on my CD player. My dad never owned a gun and never taught me to use one," Gilbert said.

"My dad was the exact opposite. He liked guns and hunting and donating to things like the red cross. I always wanted to rebel against things like that and him when I was in high school," Shannon said as she brushed back her green hair.

"Well, I don't understand who we were supposed to vote for, do you?" Rebecca changed the subject.

"You're trying to vote for a government that is more benign than malevolent toward its citizens," Zak said.

"I don't think the government is always to blame. I'm a little wary of all these good-looking people, like models and actresses. They have these seductive powers they use to get what they want without having to work hard for it," Shannon said.

"All good-looking people are enemies to humanity," Gilbert said.

Zak laughed and said, "I always felt in order to have a relationship with a good-looking woman, you have to have a James Bond-like lifestyle."

"You definitely have to know how to fight, I would think," Gilbert said.

"Or be some kind of prominent person or at least a Wall Street investor," Zak said.

"What do you think about television and this 24-7 news cycle?" Gilbert asked the girls.

"I don't like TV with an agenda. I would rather watch *The Flintstones* or *The Honeymooners*," Shannon said.

"Yeah, they used to have cool music shows like *American Bandstand* and *Soul Train*. Now it's *The Voice*," Gilbert said.

"Well, me and Gilbert decided to keep our new wave hairstyles because of the new wave revival that's going on now," Zak said.

"We're already growing tired of that," Shannon said with a blank look on her face and then smiled briefly.

Both Gilbert and Zak took this comment to heart, and Gilbert flipped her a bird. Both Rebecca and Shannon laughed, and the conversation was stalled for a second before Shannon decided to patch things up.

"We don't necessarily have to be entertained all the time. We're not too hard to please," Shannon said with a complicit smile.

Gilbert and Zak looked at each other and came to an unspoken agreement between each other that they would continue to talk to the girls.

"Aren't you a little interested in what I've learned in religious studies?" Gilbert asked Shannon.

"I've always been a little wary of religious believers, and I've never trusted preachers," Shannon said.

"Well, there are all types of religious beliefs and customs to consider, and I've learned a lot about them," Gilbert said.

"For example, do you know there's a secret room in the Vatican that has all types of pagan sculptures and texts, and there are guards there that will defend them with deadly force if needed."

"You mean just like those signs in Area 51 that say, 'Use of deadly force if necessary?'"

"I think it's just meant to scare people away," Zak said.

"I think they really mean to kill people if they try to delve too far into that place. It's all government secrets and UFOs and stuff. You know what I mean?" Gilbert said.

"What do you think of all these people getting glorified and deified for the way they are. They're admired and idolized and put on some kind of pedestal for their achievements in life," Gilbert said with a scornful look on his face.

"Do you mean politicians?" Shannon said.

"Politicians get so much slack from their opposing side. I wouldn't think he's talking about them," Rebecca said.

"Yeah, but don't they get statues and memorials about them?" Shannon said.

"I was talking more about pop stars and movies stars that win awards and accolades for their charity work," Gilbert said.

"I think one person who's been given status as a divine being is John Lennon," Zak said.

"What about all those one-hit wonders from the '80s like the *Thompson Twins* and the *Human League*?" Shannon said.

"I wouldn't consider them people who have been elevated to some kind of divine status. It's called apotheosis, by the way," Gilbert said.

"A lot of those one-hit wonders from the '80s are doing different things now. They're painters or insurance salesman," Shannon said.

"Why did you decide to keep your new wave hairstyles?" Rebecca asked Gilbert and Zak.

"We both felt it was the best period in music. You know, with the synthesizers and all that stuff," Gilbert said.

"We felt that the goths had the right idea about art, and we wanted to emulate it in our clothes and hairstyles," Rebecca spoke for both her and Shannon.

"We seem to be getting off the subject. I thought we were talking about apotheosis," Gilbert said, a little irritated.

"That's something a religious studies major like you wants to talk about. Not the rest of us," Shannon replied.

"I just thought it was an interesting topic. We ordinary citizens don't get anywhere near such status. We're the dirty and lowdown peasantry that are looked upon as second-class citizens."

"I don't think things are quite that bad, but I do remember being kicked out of certain clubs before," Rebecca said.

"I remember going to a girl's house before, and the mother kicked me out telling me, 'You weren't invited,'" Zak said.

"Were you?" Shannon said.

"No, but I still felt like a second-class citizen when she escorted me outside and told me she would call the police if I ever came back," Zak said.

"Why would you go to someone's house uninvited?" Shannon said.

"I liked her."

"That should be a good enough reason to go to someone's house. You like them," Rebecca said.

"Some people are just huffy and haughty and like to show how much of a snob they are," Gilbert said.

"I think you all need to be taught the proper social protocol," Shannon said.

"I would rather just toilet paper their lawn," Zak said. Everyone laughed except Shannon.

"How did we get to this subject anyways?" Shannon asked.

"We were talking about apotheosis," Zak said.

"The promotion of a human being to divine status?" Rebecca said.

"It's an interesting concept, but I don't think hardly anyone has heard of the word," Shannon said in her critical manner.

"I know of many saints and bishops throughout history that that word might apply to, but I think the word has taken a new meaning in the twenty-first century," Gilbert commented.

"You think that there are people who have been given that status more for their achievements rather than their religious position?" Zak asked.

"I think we've talked enough about this subject. You have our numbers, so we're probably going to leave now," Shannon said.

Gilbert looked over at Zak and motioned him to leave the table with the girls.

"I guess this is a raincheck," Gilbert said to Shannon.

Both Gilbert and Zak made their way through the crowd and out through a side door into the starlit night, with the glow of the streetlamp lighting their way home.

Daybreak at Fort Jackson

The road march came to an end back at the company's barracks near the commissary and meal hall. Shawn stood still as the drill sergeant made his final announcement to their platoon. The life of a soldier in basic training was confined to just a few buildings for the most part if you didn't include the few excursions and road marches they would go on. He looked around at some of the other members of the platoon. There were some that were clearly worn out by the road march while others that didn't seem too fazed by the day's exertion. It was ten miles which would wear out anyone over thirty, but Shawn knew these guys in this platoon were young and physically fit enough to handle such a march.

"Fall out!" Drill Sergeant Laker said as Shawn's platoon was released to the gray, dreary barracks building with its half-opened transoms and windows. Shawn made his way to the supply room at the front of the barracks building because he was assigned this duty by the drill sergeant. He was always told never to volunteer for anything by his recruiter, but if being the supply clerk would keep him out of KP, he was all for it.

He entered the supply room and looked around at the various ammo belts and ammo pouches that were strewn across the room. Shawn knew he had his work cut out for him for the night and hoped his assistant would be there shortly. His assistant was a Black kid who seemed to know what he was doing when it came to organization and taking orders. His last name was Pruett, and that is what he was called. Everyone in the platoon called each other by their last name, as that is what was embroidered on their camo shirts.

"Pennington!" Pruett called out to Shawn as he entered the supply room.

"You don't have to call me that. You can call me Shawn," Shawn said.

"How about Cap'n Shawn," Pruett said in his own brand of humor.

"If that makes you feel any better." Shawn smiled.

"So tell me, dawg, what do we have to do tonight?" Pruett said.

"Mainly getting these ammo belts and pouches organized for the marksmanship drills at the end of the week," Shawn said.

"Did these just come in?" Pruett said.

"It's not all of them, but at least we could get started," Shawn said.

They began counting the belts for the platoon, and Shawn knew the exact number of men in his platoon so that he could order the remaining ones the next day. He felt his handwriting was legible enough to fill out the supply forms. You needed a form for just about everything in the Army, and Shawn wanted him and Pruett to be on top of things.

Their platoon was known as the "snooze platoon" because of a lot of the guys drifting off in sleep during the indoor training classes. Shawn wanted to change that reputation and beat out one of the higher-achiever platoons in the company. It was run by one of the meanest and most intimidating drill sergeants he had ever known. He was a tall, White guy with eyes that could stare through your soul. He definitely kept a taught ship. Their platoon's drill sergeant ran things differently. He could get riled if need be, but he didn't rule by fear like the other platoon's sergeant. Shawn respected him, and he wanted to prove they could be the winning platoon by his drill sergeant's leadership methods.

"What should we do with these cleaning supplies?" Pruett said.

"Put them in the cleaning closet," Shawn said.

"I know that. There's just so much of it. Shouldn't we dole it out to the other platoons?" Pruett said.

"I guess so. Just make sure it doesn't go to Fisk's platoon. You know what I mean?" Shawn said.

"Gotcha, boss."

Around about six, they were able to get the ammo belts counted before mealtime. They knew once again they were going to have to hurry up and wait for chow. That was the code of the Army—hurry up and wait, hurry up and wait.

After chow, Shawn and Pruett returned to the supply room, trying to decide how to dole out the cleaning supplies to the other platoons without Fisk's platoon knowing. Pruett decided he would go to the other supply specialists himself and hand them their cleaning supplies and tell them not to mention this act of gratitude to Fisk's platoon. After a while, Pruett got to thinking about it and realized he was afraid of Fisk's platoon.

"Why should we even care if Fisk's platoon knows about it?" he asked Shawn.

"They may try something on us if they hear we snubbed them. They're a very competitive platoon," Shawn said.

"Well, I would like to snub Drill Sergeant Fisk. Just once."

"I'd advise against it. We need to keep some secrecy. I think we're finished for today. Let's go outside and take a break. It'll give us a chance to shoot the shit for a little while," Shawn said.

"I think I would like to do that with you, Pennington," Pruett answered.

They went outside and sat on the knee-length wall that separated their platoon's barracks from the neighboring one. The sun was still in the sky, and Shawn liked it when he could sit down and feel the sun on his lap. Pruett sat on one of the officer's chairs that were situated in the area. They sat for a while in silence while Pruett had a smoke. It was Pruett who began the conversation.

"What do you remember the most about home?"

"The war of the air conditioner."

Pruett laughed. "I know what you mean, man."

"You know, Drill Sergeant Fisk doesn't deserve to have the best platoon. He rules them with fear. That's not the way it should be," Pruett said.

"I've been thinking about that too, and I agree with you. He runs that platoon like it's a third-world country."

"They're always doing the best in the marksmanship ranges and marching drills. I just don't understand it," Pruett said.

"They're too damned afraid to mess up," Shawn said. "Maybe if they're barracks got a little messy and smelly because they don't have the extra cleaning supplies, it would demoralize them."

"I don't think anything we do in that respect is going to make them any lesser than the best platoon in the battalion," Pruett said.

"We can always try. You know, one time, I went off from the barracks to the PX and had to have a pass and left my pass on the bus on the way home, and Fisk caught me getting off the bus. He asked for my pass, and when I couldn't find it, he made me do thirty push-ups. The whole time he just stared at me with his glowing eyes. You know that stare he has? I felt so humiliated over a stupid little pass. I personally would like to see our platoon do better at the marksmanship ranges. Beat that guy."

"They're a lot of things about the military and war I wonder about. I've heard all types of stories of how the higher-ups got to be where they are," Pruett said.

"I guess you think by suckin' up, right?" Shawn challenged Pruett.

"Well, a lot of them had combat duty, and I wonder what kind of combat duty, you know?" Pruett said. "I mean, they ended up with a higher rank, or they ended up in Arlington, y' know?"

"A lot of them were brave and earned medals for what they did," Shawn said.

"I think a lot of them got their positions by being sneaky cowards if you ask me," Pruett said. "They knew better than going into the line of fire."

"Well, you don't want to make yourself a target," Shawn said.

"I think the brave ones that weren't cowardly are in Arlington national cemetery now," Pruett said as he began to pick the dirt off of his combat boots.

"There's really no way of knowing. You trust that the higher-ups know what they're doing," Shawn said.

"Oh, they know what they're doing all right," Pruett said.

"Let's keep our mind on the issues at hand. We've got a long way to go if we want to beat Fisk's platoon. There are going to be barracks inspections in the next couple of days. We may even see a lieutenant colonel or colonel come by," Shawn said.

"Maybe we can use our drill sergeant's leniency on us as a way to break the spirit of Fisk's platoon," Pruett said.

"What do you mean?"

"Maybe if Drill Sergeant Laker gave us a little more freedoms like listening to our tape decks at night, it would raise our morale and lower theirs," Pruett said.

"You mean if we ran a freer platoon, it would help us achieve better than Fisk's platoon?"

"You got it."

"That works in the real world, but I don't know if that's such a good idea in the military," Shawn replied.

"You mean in order to become the best platoon, you've got to be ruled with an iron hand?"

"It sure looks like it. A lot of these guys in this company are rejects and rogues. It's the only thing they understand."

"I guess we should scrap the idea of leniency then, huh?" Pruett asked.

"We already have a reputation as the snooze platoon," Shawn said.

"You know, I keep thinking the way Drill Sergeant Fisk is, and I wonder if he's like the men I used to know back home. You know, those guys that used to hunt and trap a lot. Those guys treated women kind of like the animals they would trap. They'd butter up and treat their women nice before they married them, and then once they got that wedding band on their finger, they would feel they no longer had to be so nice to them. Kind of like a form of entrapment," Pruett said.

"They felt like they didn't have to follow their vow. They had them where they wanted them," Shawn added.

"Yeah. I think a lot of those guys were that way."

"And you think Fisk maybe that way?" Shawn asked.

Pruett started to laugh.

"I don't know, man. Maybe his wife is domineering and mean to him, and that's why he's a mean drill sergeant."

"Kind of like misplaced aggression," Shawn said.

"I don't even know if he's married though."

"I don't see why anyone would want to marry that guy," Shawn said.

"It's hard understanding women and what they want. Some women go for bad guys like that. They think that's what the world needs. Women can be just as dumb as men," Pruett said.

"Well, to think that Fisk is dumb is not completely true," Shawn said.

"I know. Never underestimate the enemy," Pruett said.

"He's not exactly an enemy, just a competitor rather," Shawn said.

Pruett began to yawn as the sun sunk in the distant horizon beyond the Army barracks. The two talked and debated about the various subjects that would arise in a Fort Jackson Company before deciding to retire for the night and resting their heads on the hard Army pillows and cots of the Fort Jackson Army base.

Fallout Shelter

The time on the infinity clock was 3:30 p.m., and Jasmine knew better than to doubt its workings. His job at the shelter was to keep an eye out for the food provisions that were stocked in the food warehouse. There were a variety of boxes and containers that were the sustenance of this fallout shelter: the only place Jasmine knew throughout his lifespan.

He never had memories of a different life somewhere else. He didn't know who his parents were; all he knew was that he had duties to fulfill and that the place he lived in, the fallout shelter, was meant to protect him and his "family" from the evil that existed on the outside. The outside was full of dangerous toxins and lifelessness with no law and order to speak of. He felt secure and glad he was being taken care of by the "family."

Most of the warehouse and the many rooms of the shelter were dark, shadowy places. The lighting was not the best because of the conservation methods used by the shelter. He knew the shelter was powered by a fusion power source deep within its structure. All he knew were that his duties were to keep an eye out and work as a manager for the food storehouse. Keeping track of the colony's food was his priority task.

As he walked down the rows and rows of boxes of food, he had to keep inventory on what was available to eat and how much longer it would last. The boxes of MREs (meals, ready to eat) would not last as long as the boxes of food that took some kind of boiling water to make. He knew the MREs were at one time made by the outside military and didn't have a long shelf life, but Jasmine personally preferred the other type of food that was boiled in water.

As he was doing his inventory, he heard the sound of shuffling behind him. At first, he suspected it was an intruder, but then he heard a voice.

"Jasmine, Jasmine, are you almost finished?"

It was Jales. Jales was a fellow member of the "family" and was in charge of what was called Workload. He had to keep tabs on everyone's duties and distribute work to everyone in a way that was equal and fair—or at least equal and fair according to the dictates of the "family."

"Jales, you know I won't be finished for another hour or two."

"If it's for the family, I would think it's all right, but if you're just fiddle-faddlin' for yourself, then I take issue with it," Jales said.

"I do what's best for the colony and nothing more," Jasmine replied.

"Well, make sure you fill out the necessary sections in your workbook before you turn it in to me."

"Why is it so necessary to fill out our personal workbook all the time?" Jasmine asked.

"It's not your place to ask such questions. Serving the colony is what is most important," Jales snapped.

"All right. But that might take a little extra time. I'll try to fit it in as best as I can."

Jasmine had noticed Jales was taller and more weighty than he was, but that never bothered him. He knew everyone's duties were assigned to them because that was what they were mostly cut out to do. There was the board that handled such matters, but he didn't know much about that. All he knew were some of his fellow compatriots and his educator, Ms. O'Toole.

Jasmine made his way back to the food storage warehouse and reached into a box and pulled out an MRE and shoved it into his pocket. He felt this act of rebellion was necessary, considering Jales's curt attitude toward him was unnecessary. He would just write the MRE off on his inventory roster.

As he finished his rounds of counting the food inventory, he made his way back to where Jales was. He had a friendship of sorts with Jales, but they seemed to be at odds about things Jasmine wasn't sure he could fully explain yet. When he reached a small well-lit room, he saw Jales standing with one of those computer pads in his hand that he wished he had.

"I finished the inventory. Are you still having to do your work?" Jasmine asked Jales.

"I'll be finished with the duty roster here in a second," Jales said.

Jasmine noticed that Jales had connections to the board and took orders directly from them, unlike himself and some of the other members of the colony. Jasmine never really cared if he had such access to the higher members of the "family." He didn't let himself be bothered too much by it or let it get in the way of his duties.

"Do you think I will ever get to use one of those pads?"

"These pads are solely for the ones selected to use the pads. The board picks them as a special group that can be trusted," Jales said.

"You made the cut then," Jasmine said.

"In a way," Jales said in an offhanded way without looking into Jasmine's eyes.

There was an awkward silence between the two when Jales decided to break it just to make Jasmine more comfortable.

"Are you learning anything in Ms. O'Toole's class?"

"She's taught me a lot about computers. What I don't understand are the social engineering goals they want us to understand. I get all confused."

"Eventually, all those clouds will clear away, and you'll see everything the way it's supposed to be seen," Jales said.

"Do you understand everything they talk about?"

"Of course. I'm a model member of the colony. That's why I have a pad to account for everyone's work duties. I'm in charge of Workload, remember?"

Jasmine was silent but decided to shift the conversation to something else.

"When are we having the annual celebration of the fallout shelter this year?"

"You mean tribute day?" Jales countered with a question he didn't expect to be answered. He gave a knowing smile and answered it himself.

"It's scheduled for three weeks from now. I know all about the festivities and how they will be conducted. I'm in charge of Workload, remember?"

"Do you think there will be a dance this year?"

"The board still believes that music should be illegal. Where did you learn about dancing?" Jales asked.

"Ms. O'Toole talked about it," Jasmine lied.

Jasmine was a good reader, and he had frequented the library to see what kind of books were there. It was only a couple of shelves of books from what he remembered. There were a lot of how-to books and books on Marxist thought, but he managed to find a book that had slipped behind the shelves and was stuck in between the wall and shelving that had a word he didn't know: an encyclopedia.

Jasmine wondered if the book was there by mistake or if someone had placed it there. This was the book that told him about dancing. He decided if the matter was brought up by Jales to Ms. O'Toole, he would lie and say he got it from one of the how-to books. He felt he was reading something he wasn't supposed to be reading and didn't want them to know about it.

"How many more years before I get promoted to a better job, do you think?" Jasmine asked Jales.

"You'll have to prove your loyalty to the colony. You haven't really done that enough yet. The family has strict vetting procedures before you're allowed to get things like a pad or enter the inner sanctum."

"The inner sanctum? What's that?"

"I can't tell you too much, but you're supposed to bow down to one of the members of the board in this secretive room, profess your loyalty, and answer certain crucial questions in order to enter the colony's upper tier. I've probably told you too much already," Jales said.

"It sounds kind of scary."

"It's supposed to be," Jales answered. "Don't ask me any more questions about that. We have work to do."

Jales began to look irritated talking about the subject and resumed his log work on his pad. Jasmine decided not to push him for any more questions about the inner workings of the colony. He was beginning to learn the skill of when to hold back to these people and not to press them about things. It was a very useful skill indeed, and it helped him in a lot of ways.

"Well, I've got to make my way back to the food warehouse. I'll see you," Jasmine said as he walked down the dimly lit corridor to his workstation.

He hoped it didn't seem like he was breaking off communication with Jales too abruptly as he really wished to eat the stolen MRE. As he had walked a good distance down the corridor, he decided he was out of sight and earshot of Jales and reached into his cargo pocket and drew out the MRE. All he knew was that he was always hungry with all the work he did for the colony. He used his pocketknife to open it and noticed he got the franks and beans dinner. He ate it with no regret that it was stolen.

He made his way back to the food warehouse and sat down at a table and chairs and finished the MRE. He licked his salty fingers from the MRE crackers and wondered if they would ever find out about his robbing of the food warehouse. He tried his best to write it off of his log and inventory but always felt there might be a way they could find out. He sat back in his chair, thinking about the day's activities and his conversations with Jales and slowly began to doze off.

* * *

Ms. O'Toole's class was a small one, with only seven students. Jasmine sat in the back, but Ms. O'Toole would call on him for answers to questions every so often. Jasmine would rather she left him alone, but he decided she was just trying to educate him as well as the others.

"Jasmine, what have you learned in this class?" Ms. O'Toole said.

"Well, you talk about how the world outside used to oppress and subjugate women. Then you mention the New Dawn that our colony represents that will do things differently."

"Very good, Jasmine. You know, I once was married until the fallout shelter showed me the error of my ways. I once was a Mrs. O'Toole, but now I am a Ms. O'Toole, an independent woman who follows the dictates of the colony now."

"Are there any women in the colony who are married?" Jasmine asked.

"It is not your place to ask questions like that," Ms. O'Toole said.

Ms. O'Toole turned back to the class and asked everyone to recite the various Marxist sayings that were inscribed in their primer. Everyone joined in, with Jasmine mumbling them as best as he could. Jasmine had read in the encyclopedia he found that primers were supposed to teach the alphabet and arithmetic, but all these primers seemed to teach were computer iconography. He wondered if anyone else in the classroom knew how to read like he did. He didn't know how he was literate, but he decided to keep it a secret from his teachers and the colony like the way the encyclopedia was secretly hidden behind the bookcase. That seemed to be a secret that someone worked to keep, so he felt he could keep one of his own.

"Jasmine? What does this mean?" Ms. O'Toole asked.

She drew an icon on the chalkboard, hoping to challenge Jasmine in some way. Jasmine knew right away what it was but decided to act like he wasn't sure. He worked to keep Ms. O'Toole in the dark about his intellectual capabilities, so he acted like he had a hard time with the answer.

"A search icon?" Jasmine said as the others laughed.

"No, Jasmine, this is a share icon. You want to be able to share with others, don't you?"

"Yes, ma'am."

"Learning computer iconography is one of the most important things you can learn. Agreed, class?"

"Yes, Ms. O'Toole," said the other students collectively.

"Now, Jasmine, I know you can do better than this, but you do seem a little challenged, so I will work with you on the iconography," Ms. O'Toole said.

Jasmine barely shook his head in agreement. He knew keeping the fact that he understood how to read English, and the English alphabet from Ms. O'Toole might prove to be a difficult task in the future.

Ms. O'Toole disbanded the class after giving an announcement of the duties the students would have for the upcoming tribute day. As the students walked out, Ms. O'Toole called out for Jasmine as he was about to leave. Jasmine reluctantly walked over to her desk.

"Jasmine, I think you could do as well as the other students if you would just apply yourself. I know this iconography can be challenging, but you should catch up with the other students if you try."

"I'm doing my best," Jasmine lied.

"Well, I know you could do better and maybe get a higher position in your work duties than just food service," Ms. O'Toole suggested to Jasmine in a way that reminded him of Jales. "You know, this colony was formed to protect the young from the ravages of the world that used to be." Ms. O'Toole continued, "Your fellow citizens believed in competing against each other to the point where they made a mess of the world they created. People could no longer breathe the air and drink the water. Strains of disease and pestilence were rampant. We don't want our young to be raised in the same way they used to be raised. We want everyone to realize they are equal and should remain equal. To grow and achieve is a thing of the past. Do you understand, Jasmine?"

"Yes, Ms. O'Toole," Jasmine mumbled.

"Now let's see you learn that iconography the same as the other students so that you can be equal to them."

Jasmine held his head down and acted like he was dejected as he walked out of the classroom. As he made his way down the dimly lit hallway, he wasn't worried at all about the memorization of computer icons. He decided to try to please Ms. O'Toole by showing that he could be "equal" to the others even though he was sure he was the only one in the class that could read English.

The boxes were heavy, but Jasmine did his best to load them on the delivery cart that would take them to the main cafeteria. The colony's leaders told everyone in the fallout shelter that work helps with your self-esteem, but Jasmine always felt he could be doing something better than what he was doing. He didn't feel working below your station in life was any help to his self-esteem.

As soon as he was finished with the food loading, he knew it was up to him to deliver the carts to the main cafeteria. This was a little bit more of a fun job since the delivery carts were motorized, and he could drive them down the long tunnels that the fallout shelter was made up of. He hoped to get a break after his deliveries to regroup his mind and think about the things Jales said. He wasn't sure if Jales was literate or if members of the board were.

He thought about it sometimes.

The trek through the tunnels used to scare him, but he was getting used to it now. He kept telling himself he had an important job, so he shouldn't mind all the drudgery that went along with it. The lights of the tunnel would flash their beams on his delivery cart every so often as he made his way through the tunnel. He pulled out another MRE and then thought twice about eating it as the cafeteria came into view.

Waiting at the entrance to the cafeteria were two people that Jasmine didn't recognize and Jales. As soon as he drove his delivery cart up to them, one of the unknown men put his hand on the cart as if wanting Jasmine to come to a halt with it.

"Are you Jasmine, the food service worker?" the man said as he gripped the delivery cart.

"Yes, that's me," Jasmine said.

"We need to talk with you about an infringement," the man said. "Could you please step out of the delivery cart and empty your pockets."

Jasmine, with a look of shock on his face, stepped out of the delivery cart and emptied his pockets unto the ground. All he had were two MREs in his two cargo pockets.

Both men looked at each other as Jales shook his head in disappointment. Jasmine stood standing there with a look of disgust on his face.

"It's unfortunate, but you will have to face the board for this," the man in authority said. "It's a violation of colony code 2-53, theft of food essentials."

The other man took out a pair of plastic restraints and made Jasmine turn around as he tied them on Jasmine's hands. Jasmine stared at the ground as Jales shook his head in disapproval. The other man put his hand on Jasmine's shoulder and squeezed.

"This is for your own good, son."

Jasmine stared at the cell door, watching the shadows of the people beyond it. He had no idea what was next for him. His thought was they were going to put him in front of some board of authority figures or maybe interrogate him. He had been waiting in his cell now for twelve hours. It was cold, dark, and dank in the cell, and Jasmine was wondering when they were going to feed him. He thought maybe they weren't feeding him to try to teach him a lesson.

As he sat debating the reasons for his imprisonment, the clank of the door from the outside made Jasmine realize they were finally going to send someone inside with him.

Jasmine recognized the man that walked in as the man that first served him with the charges. He was a tall, towering figure with a clean-shaven look about him. He seemed to have a sullen, somber demeanor when he began to speak to Jasmine.

"Are you aware of the seriousness of your violation?"

"I was hungry," Jasmine said.

"That's beside the point. A very serious infringement of food law was made. We're not sure yet how we will hand down a punishment. We're beginning to check inventory to discover the number of food meals stolen and subtract that amount from your colony allotment. This we feel will be the proper punishment. You may be hungry for a couple of days, but you will learn your lesson. By the way, my name is Ron."

"I felt I deserved more because I work very hard for food service."

"You shouldn't want more than the others. It's all a part of our mission of equality for the colony," Ron said.

"If someone works harder than the others, shouldn't they receive more?"

"You're testing my patience, Jasmine. I suggest you adhere to the rules of the colony or face more severe punishment."

Jasmine paused for a few moments, thinking of what to say next that wouldn't offend the enforcer.

"I don't feel completely happy with my position in the colony. Maybe if I got a better staff position, I would like it more."

Jasmine knew this was a shot in the dark since he was the only one they had that was willing to do the work he was currently doing. He knew he was smarter than the other young workers but was given more menial jobs.

"You're in no position to bargain with us at this time. We are the ones that are calling the shots here. Once you've shown us a satisfactory work performance, you might be able to bargain for another position," Ron said.

Jasmine decided to remain silent and not speak to the enforcer in fear of offending him further. He waited for Ron to speak.

"Well, we'll keep you in meditative isolation until we decide on any further punishment you will receive," the enforcer said.

The enforcer got up from the chair and knocked on the cell door, signaling to the outside guards to open them. Jasmine stared at Ron with a look of disgust on his face. He knew there was not much more to say about his situation and confinement.

He began to regain his strength when they finally started feeding him again. He wondered if the punishment Ron talked about was what was being enforced on him. He couldn't remember how many meals he missed compared to the number of meals he had stolen, but he knew they were not going to starve him to death. He thought maybe they would forego certain meals at times and then feed him at others until he had paid back his restitution.

As he sat in his cell, he tried ways to fight his depression by thinking of things he had learned in the library. He remembered Latin conjugation tables and would rattle them off in his head. He would also go through the multiplication tables he had learned in a math book he was reading.

As he tried to keep his mind occupied, a light appeared in the cell door window, making him think there was some unknown visitor outside. Just when his thoughts were beginning to uplift, the outside door closed, and the cell door light went out. He wondered what it was all about when he looked at the floor and saw an envelope. The person on the outside must have slipped it under the door.

He picked up the envelope and opened it. Inside was a note:

> I don't know why I'm doing this, but I feel you need the help. I don't know what's in store for you in the colony, but it doesn't look good. I am writing you to let you know there is a way to escape out of that cell and the colony. There are ducts that can be accessed through the cell ceiling, and with a little climbing, you can climb the ducts out of the colony to the outside world. Being a member of the board, I am literate and able to write this note to you. Don't ask me how I know that you're literate. I don't know why you would want to go outside, but this is your chance. I personally would never consider it.
>
> Good luck,
> J

It was Jales!

Jasmine read the note in disbelief and wondered about the risks Jales had to make to get this to him. He was surprised to hear that Jales knew he was literate. How he knew he did not know. He crumpled up the letter and decided to put it in his pocket. He decided it might be best not to waste any more time and try to look for the ducts Jales was talking about.

"I can't believe I'm having to do this," Jasmine said aloud to himself.

He began looking at the ceiling for any signs of holes or loose ceiling tiles where the duct could be behind. Luckily, there was plenty of light in the room, and he knew it would be a couple of hours before the lights were turned off for the night. It was easy to move around the cot until he might eventually find the duct.

He got on top of the cot and felt around the ceiling where the cot was currently positioned under. His height was tall enough to test the ceiling tiles and see if they were loose. He knew this might go on for a while.

As he continued to position the cot in different places in the room looking for an opening, he was about to give up on the task when he noticed a hole in a corner tile. He moved the cot below the tile and stood on the cot. With his outstretched hand, he lifted the tile off of the opening and stared with disbelief at the gaping maw of a tunnel going parallel to the ceiling and the floor and clearly leading out of his cell.

Jales was right!

He knew it wouldn't be too long before the guards in the cell would begin to notice something was wrong, so he decided to go ahead and hoist himself up in the tunnel. As he did so, he noticed a musty smell and was almost afraid he was going to sneeze and give himself away, but soon his whole torso was in the tunnel, and with a final heave, he pulled his legs onto the duct over the ceiling.

As he lay in the duct, a wave of doubt came over him as he thought about his escape. Was Jales telling him the truth about the duct leading to the outside? Or was he lying about it to get him into trouble? More importantly, what lay on the outside? Was it all just fallout and desolation? How would he survive? He knew he didn't have too much time to think about it and began to shimmy his way through the duct.

At first, the going was easy as he slowly worked his way through the horizontal duct. He knew he wasn't claustrophobic but began breathing hard as he started thinking of the enforcers of the colony and whether they would find out about his escape. Would there be an alarm rung soon? When would be the next time they would check his cell room? Would he be safely away from the shelter by then?

As he was thinking of these things, other difficulties began to arise. The duct took a different angle, and Jasmine had to start holding his hands and feet against the duct and working his way up. His breathing became harder, and he was uncertain how long he would have to traverse the duct this way. He decided to wipe his worries out of his brain and focus on getting through the tunnel.

Just when he thought he couldn't make the diagonal ascent, Jasmine could see up ahead that the duct took a horizontal angle once again. With every bit of his strength, he shimmied up the duct until he made it to the horizontal lip of the duct and took a jump that landed his torso unto the upper part of the tunnel. For a minute, he lay on the tunnel to catch his breath. He wondered if the worst was over or if he would have more climbing to do. He looked down the tunnel and saw a ray of light shining into the tunnel from above. He realized this might be the way out. He got up on his feet and began to walk with his back bent to the ray of light.

As he made it to the spot where the ray of light was, he reached out his hand to where the light shone and looked at his hand as the light shone on it. He seemed slightly amazed and relieved as he turned his hand over and over while the light shone on it. He looked up and saw a grill with the sunlight behind it, which must have been the source of light. It was then in the dark that he detected what looked like rungs on a ladder built into the wall leading up to the grill.

He had found what might be his escape!

He began to worry about what might be on the outside. Would there be a chance to survive on the outside? He was told all there were was fallout, desolation, and wild beasts. The war of long ago left the outside uninhabitable for any member of the colony.

As he stood there, shaking from the cold of the duct, he realized there was no turning back to the days of the colony anymore and that whatever lay before him on the outside was the fate he would have to take. He took a deep breath and started to climb the ladder. He decided it was easy enough to make it up the ladder but wondered if he would have a hard time opening the mesh at the top that led to the outside.

When he reached the top, he looked at the mesh and realized the screws that held it were loose. With his long fingernails, he knew he could possibly loosen them. Knowing that you turn them in a left-most fashion to loosen them he had discovered in a how-to book he had read, he began to try to loosen them. At first, it was difficult loosening them with his fingernails, but eventually, the third was pried loose, and Jasmine swiveled the mesh on its final screw and was able to make an opening to the outside for him to climb through.

He hoisted himself unto the opening, and with just a few grunts, he was outside. The daylight was piercing his eyes, and for a while, he seemed temporarily blinded, but as his eyes adjusted to what was around him, he became exhilarated by the outside air and sunshine, and he wasn't as fearful of the outside like he once was.

He looked around him and noticed his escape hatch was part of some kind of alcove built into the ground that led underground. He noticed behind this alcove was what looked like an alleyway between two deserted buildings that led to some kind of town square. Jasmine decided to follow it and see where it led to.

As he began to walk down the deserted alleyway in the distance, he could see people dressed in nice clothes going about what looked like regular town business. It was then that he began to realize all of what the colony told him about the outside was wrong.

He had been fooled!

He saw the smiles and eager looks of what looked like the younger folk going to what must have been their classes in some kind of local university. They were dressed well and looked happy at what they were doing. He wondered about his own situation and why he was kept in the dark about what was really on the outside. There was no fallout! There was no desolation! The only conclusion he could make about his origins was that he must have been some member of an underprivileged class that this society decided to put in their closet. He was some kind of plebeian who was lied to about his world and his own situation in the world.

These revelations left him a little disheartened, but he was determined not to go back. He had heard of "soup kitchens" and decided that was what he would find first before he broke his story to this brave new world. He wasn't sure if this would be a good idea or if even this outside world would consider it newsworthy or not.

As he walked down Town Square Street, he began to realize what he needed to do. It would be in his best interest if he just "faded into the woodwork" in this outside society. Maybe take on menial jobs in the neighborhood and eventually procure a place to live without raising any eyebrows from people. He was young and smart and could possibly succeed in some way on the outside but in a way that would give the security of shadows. With these thoughts, Jasmine felt confident enough to make it in this bold new world.

About the Author

Kirk Andersen was born in Chicago, Illinois, but his family moved to Athens, Tennessee, when he was twelve years old. He graduated from McMinn County High School without getting into too much trouble. He did a two-year stint in the US Army and then attended college at the University of Tennessee, Knoxville, for four years with a major in journalism before dropping out. Kirk Andersen now lives in Athens, Tennessee with his autistic brother and his collection of 800 boardgames. Besides having a hobby in reading books and writing, he plays and designs board games as well.

CPSIA information can be obtained
at www.ICGtesting.com
Printed in the USA
LVHW100828150123
737078LV00001B/1